# OF OWL THE NERVE

## OWL STAR WITCH MYSTERIES BOOK 13

### LEANNE LEEDS

Of Owl the Nerve
ISBN: 978-1-950505-87-6
Published by Badchen Publishing
14125 W State Highway 29
Suite B-203 119
Liberty Hill, TX 78642 USA

# CONTENTS

# OF OWL THE NERVE

# CHAPTER ONE

*I* rummaged through the cluttered mess in my bedroom, tripping over the unfamiliar silver heels Emma had insisted I wear as maid of honor. Where had I put that stupid matching purse?

"Hurry up, Astra!" Archie hooted from the windowsill. "You're already running fifteen minutes behind."

I grumbled, not used to wearing shoes that could double as medieval torture devices or keeping to the tight schedule Emma had mapped out for her wedding week festivities. When I agreed to be Emma's maid of honor, I never imagined how much preparation, stress, and perfectly timed coordination would be involved in a human wedding.

And here was the kicker: this wasn't even a standard, run-of-the-mill human wedding.

In this marriage extravaganza, the groom was a werewolf, the ring bearer a younger version of the same, one of the co-best men was a card-carrying vampire, and the entire bridal party, excluding the bride, were bona fide witches. With all the magic swirling around, we could have simply enchanted a broomstick, had them leap over it, and called it a day.

But no.

Emma wanted a human wedding.

My usual disciplined but heavily casual approach to life hadn't been meshing well with the multitude of appointments, fittings, cake tastings, and everything else on Emma's extensive checklist.

After stubbing my toe for the third time, I finally spotted my purse peeking from under the bed skirt. "Aha!" I snatched it up in triumph, only to hear Archie screech again.

"Come on, come on! Rehearsal dinner starts in ten minutes, and you know how Emma gets when anyone's late for this wedding garbage."

"Keep your feathers on. I'm coming," I

grumbled. I rubbed my sore toe, wondering how I'd survive this wedding in one piece, and then hastened out of the bedroom with a final glance in the mirror to make sure I looked presentable. Who knew being in a wedding could be so hazardous to your health?

I clambered down the stairs as quickly as my pinching heels would allow, nearly tumbling into my sisters gathered at the bottom.

"There you are!" Thea exclaimed. "We were about to send out a search party."

Ami ran her fingers over the delicate fabric of her pale dress and then handed me my matching coat from the closet. "You're usually not this tardy. Wedding jitters getting to you already?"

"What would I have jitters about? It's not my wedding. More like shoe jitters." I waved at my silver heels before stepping forward with a wince. "How do you walk in these knee-breakers, Ami?"

My psychic sibling merely shrugged, far more acclimated to the attire of dresses and heels than I was. Ami's elegant, flowing gown, complemented by strappy silver sandals, matched her graceful, gentle demeanor. On the other hand, I felt as graceful as a gangly newborn giraffe in my designated attire.

Ayla descended the stairs last, her gauzy black

dress nearly catching on the banister posts. My youngest sister patted around the pockets of her dress, which was really more appropriate for a spooky séance than a wedding rehearsal. "Aunt Gertie said Melvin just texted me. Has anyone seen my phone?"

"Forget about Melvin—or your phone—for now. We have to go! And frankly, Astra, maybe you better let me drive. You might get that shoe all tangled up on the gas pedal." Thea herded us out the front door toward the driveway where my Jeep was parked. No sooner had I slipped into the backseat beside Ami than Thea peeled out of the driveway, tires squealing.

"Easy, Thea!" I braced myself against the door as we careened down the street. Between Thea's maniacal driving and these treacherous shoes, I might not make it to the wedding at this rate.

Some maid of honor I was turning out to be.

Especially considering most of us were sure this wedding would never happen.

Emma had always kept Eddie on his toes, that was for sure. Since they reconnected, the alpha werewolf had chased after Emma, lavishing her with affection, planning elaborate dates and surprises to sweep her off her feet—but Emma had always held back, keeping Eddie at arm's length for reasons I never entirely understood.

But I was also not one to talk.

So I didn't.

It wasn't that she didn't love the man—any fool could see the adoration in her eyes when she looked at Eddie. My best friend wasn't a cruel woman, but I'd swear she seemed to enjoy emotionally torturing poor Eddie, moving toward him slowly and then pulling back at the last second.

When Eddie swallowed his pride and took another swing at proposing to Emma, it was like a curveball coming right out of left field. I was thrown for a loop, just like the rest of our ragtag crew. We'd assumed he'd given up. I mean, most of us would have.

And then it came.

The word we'd been waiting for.

"Yes."

She breathed out the word, a single syllable so ripe with promise it could have filled a whole library of love stories. The next thing I knew, we were transforming that weird werewolf castle into a wedding venue that could've given any royal shindig a run for its money.

No expense had been spared for Emma's special day—or the special days leading up to the special day. Eddie had moved mountains to make this the wedding of Emma's dreams, and what mountains Eddie couldn't move, Emma's hulking linebacker-built father or vampire brother did.

Hopefully, after so many years of waiting, Emma had finally realized what a gem she had in Eddie, and the two would get the happily ever after they—and Hunter—deserved.

* * *

THEA SCREECHED into the parking lot of Sanguine, the upscale nightclub owned by Emma's vampire brother, Rex Sullivan. Even though the club was closed for the private rehearsal dinner, the building was aglow, with strands of pink and white twinkle lights winding around the entrance and spotlighting a handmade sign announcing the rehearsal dinner above.

My heels clicked across the pavement as I followed my sisters inside, and as the doors swung open, I felt like we had walked straight into a cotton candy dream. The scene before us was all soft pastels and shimmering glitter, so sweet and effervescent it might as well have been spun from sugar and fairy dust, draped in Emma's (temporarily) favorite colors with bridal accents at every turn.

Usually, the club sported a… well, if you've ever pictured a vampire-themed color palette, that's how it was decorated, and this was about as far off as you could get.

It was less 'midnight crypt' and more 'midday unicorn parade.'

A blond blur rocketed toward me in a flurry of tulle and lace. "Astra, there you are!" Emma threw her arms around me. "I was afraid you wouldn't make it."

"And miss all this?" I gestured at the elaborate decor around us. "Not a chance. I just, uh, had some issues with my shoes. And my sisters' driving." I grimaced, flexing my toes in my dreaded high heels.

Emma's gaze swept over my ensemble with a critical eye. "You look perfect. Now come on, you're seated at the head table with me. We have a schedule to keep!" Linking her arm through mine, Emma guided me toward the front of the club, where a long table draped in pale silk and dotted with gold bud vases awaited us.

Name cards in looping calligraphy marked each seat. Emma tucked me near the center, with her mother on one side of me and one of Eddie's best men, the charming werewolf Lothian, assigned to the other. Eddie himself sat on my right, one seat away, while Rex hovered behind us.

"Where's your dad?" I asked Emma as servers appeared with salads and glasses of champagne.

A tiny crease formed between Emma's brows. "You know, I'm not sure. But don't worry—he'll be here. He knows how much this dinner means to me."

Leaning in with conspiratorial flair, Elizabeth Sullivan, Emma's mother, complimented me on my dress. "That color looks lovely on you, Astra. So flattering." A good-natured chuckle escaped her, the sound resembling that of wind chimes on a breezy afternoon. "Come to think of it, I don't think I've ever seen you in a dress before, Astra Arden."

"Oh, you can bet your last cookie you've never seen me in a dress before."

"Don't joke about last cookies. You'll give Emma a heart attack if she thinks we've run out of anything."

I chuckled. "Sorry. But thank you, Mrs.

Sullivan. Though between us, I never thought Emma would ask me to wear something like this unless we were going undercover to investigate drug sales at weddings."

Elizabeth laughed, patting my arm. "Oh, don't I know it. My Emma is a lot like her father, Thomas—tough as nails on the outside, but deep down, she's a big squishy romantic creampuff. She looks like a princess, doesn't she?"

I nodded in agreement, though I had difficulty picturing Emma's stern former high school football coach father as a "squishy creampuff."

From what I heard from Rex, Coach Sullivan had terrified half the student body back in the day with his bellowing voice and stern demeanor. Emma seemed to have inherited more of his outward toughness, though she reserved her softer side for Hunter, close friends, and—apparently—weddings.

As servers cleared the salad plates, Emma stood and clinked her champagne glass, drawing all eyes to the head table. Her gaze met mine, and for a second, I saw a flicker of apprehension in those eyes. But her smile never faltered. "Thank you all for being here to celebrate this special night with Eddie and me."

"As you, our family, know, we've had a bit of a

winding road to get here. But Eddie, you have been by my side through all the ups and downs, never wavering in your love and support. You're my best friend, the man who knows me better than anyone else." Emma blinked back tears, taking Eddie's hand. "I cannot wait to become your wife." She held up her champagne flute. "To many more adventures together!"

A chorus of cheers and applause erupted through the club. Eddie rose and pulled Emma into a sweet embrace, kissing her cheek. My eyes grew suspiciously misty.

This shindig was shaping up to be an emotional roller coaster. No two ways about it.

As Emma and Eddie retook their seats amid congratulations from all sides, I noticed her gaze straying anxiously to the club entrance again. The seat on her other side, meant for her father, remained empty.

Where was Coach Sullivan?

* * *

REX'S VOICE, a low murmur barely audible above the chatting wedding guest din, fluttered into my ear as the lights in the club dimmed, "I tried to talk him out of this. I tried. I did my best to reason with him. Honestly, I did. Everything short of hypnotizing the guy with my glamour."

"What do you mean? You tried to stop who?" Rex's embarrassment twinkled like a disco ball as he tried to distance himself from whatever impending disaster he foresaw.

"Oh, god, here he goes."

Before I could ask him again what he was talking about, the club's speakers belched out a sound that had more kick than a mule on hot asphalt. A hearty twang reverberated through the club, a noise so unapologetically country it could've knocked a cowboy off his saddle.

> Hey there, darling, it's your old man
>     standing here,
> I was a coach, you're a cop, in a field
>     of fear.
> My gridiron lessons, your
>     childhood hymns,
> Turned you into a woman stronger
>     than any gym.

"I should have bit him," Rex hissed.

The vampire cringed as Coach Sullivan

launched into the chorus of his original country and western ode to Emma, complete with exaggerated arm gestures and hip gyrations many of us probably didn't even know her father was capable of until this night.

> Now you wear that badge and
>     protect us all,
> You grew up tough, you grew up
>     tall.
> I remember teaching you to tackle
>     and to throw,
> Never thought you'd use that
>     strength to fight the foe.

I sat frozen in my seat, champagne glass halfway to my lips, unable to do anything but stare in disbelief as the burly, usually stern man pranced around the club with a microphone in hand.

I glanced at Rex, who had turned a peculiar shade of grayish-green.

> My gridiron girl, with a heart of
>     gold,
> You're tougher than the toughest I
>     have ever told.

From the football field to the city
    beat,
You're the bravest soul any danger
    could meet.

The song lumbered on for another excruciating verse and chorus.

Here's to you, my darling, as you
    start this dance,
Your life's next chapter, a new
    romance.
May your love be as strong as the
    blue in your line,
May it be as enduring, as timeless as
    thine.

Coach Sullivan ended his serenade with a dramatic bow, the club erupting into hesitant applause and laughter. Emma rose on wobbly legs and threw her arms around her father, both wiping at their eyes.

I moved closer to Rex, lowering my voice and reassuring him, "It wasn't that bad."

Rex grimaced and looked at me as if he'd bitten into a lemon thinking it was an apple. "I told him a song wasn't the best idea. But you know how he is once he gets an idea. Just like her." He rubbed his temples with a soft groan. "I don't know if I'll ever recover from the secondhand embarrassment."

"Look on the bright side. At least he didn't dance much."

My attempt at humor elicited a pained chuckle from Rex.

Coach Sullivan approached our table, pulling Elizabeth into his arms with a proud smile. "I told you the surprise would blow you away."

Elizabeth, Coach Sullivan's other half, playfully swatted at his arm. "Darling, you're a piece of work, you know that?" Her voice was all sugar and spice, with a dash of sass. "A one-man spectacle. A stand-up comedy and a circus rolled into one."

"Aw, I just wanted to do something special for my little girl. Can't a father sing at his only daughter's wedding rehearsal?" Coach Sullivan blinked innocently, though the mischievous glint in his eyes gave him away.

Emma leaned over and kissed her father's scruffy cheek. "I wouldn't have it any other way.

"Even if it was the cheesiest, corniest, most face-palm-inducing song in the annals of ever?"

Rex chimed in, his eyebrow raised in mock skepticism.

Emma's laughter rang out, clear and bright, mingling harmoniously with Rex's throaty chuckle. "Oh, Rex," she chided, her words carrying the lighthearted tease of a sibling rivalry as old as their shared history. "You're just sour because Dad didn't pen a ballad about your awesomeness. I see how it is."

"Right."

She playfully flicked a glance his way, her eyes sparkling with mirth. "Though, you should know, green with envy doesn't suit you nearly as well as your usual smug aura, dear brother."

Watching Emma and Coach Sullivan, I felt a pang of wistfulness for the relationship I'd never have with my own father. But seeing the two of them, I could pretend for a moment I understood what it felt like to have that kind of unconditional, playful love in your life.

Coach Sullivan might drive Emma up the wall at times, but he was also her rock, her hero, the man who had always been there for her no matter what. And now here he was, just days before giving his only daughter away, willing to make a complete fool of himself just to see her smile and hear her laugh for him one more time.

Yep.

An emotional roller coaster.

And we hadn't even made it to the actual wedding yet.

# CHAPTER TWO

Uncle Albert reached into the silver platter, grabbed a golden crab puff, and popped it into his mouth. His thick, white mustache quivered as he chewed, bits of flaky pastry clinging to the ends like tiny cotton balls. He swallowed with a satisfied grunt, then waved an index finger. "Your friend Emma, now there's a good girl. So well-behaved, always doing as she's told."

I stared at Emma's Uncle Albert in silence, wondering who he was talking about. Always doing as she's told?

Emma Sullivan?

Not likely.

"Not like that wayward other niece of mine,

Bea. Honestly, I don't know where we went wrong with that one. Tried to bring her up right, but she just wasn't having it."

He reached for a bacon-wrapped asparagus spear, waving it at me without regard for what was dripping off the ends. His fingers were coated in butter and sparkling with pork grease. I tried not to cringe at the sight of butter and bacon grease dripping down his chin.

"Oh, did you raise her?" I asked politely.

"No, my sister did—until that finally killed her —but since I didn't have a wife or children of my own, I helped before and after. My brother Thomas raised Emma right, with discipline and respect. Didn't need any help." Uncle Albert sighed wistfully. "Instead, I got stuck with Beatrice's nonsense and backtalk. No wonder the girl ended up in so much trouble."

Uncle Albert never married?

I couldn't imagine why.

What woman wouldn't jump at the chance to marry this ungroomed, unkempt slob that had an insult and a judgment for everyone?

"I'm sure your niece Beatrice is a wonderful woman." I gave what I hoped was an understanding smile, though, in truth, Uncle

Albert's complaining and judgmental attitude were grating on my nerves. It made me miss Archie and his talent for extricating me from situations I didn't want to be in (by swooping at people I didn't like) even more. "Is she here for Emma's wedding?"

Albert laughed. "Of course she is. She'd never miss all the free food and drink." His eyes lit up as he noticed a server passing by with a platter of brightly-colored appetizers. With lightning speed, he snatched the closest morsel—a coconut shrimp—and shoved it into his mouth before continuing on with his conversation. "She's probably over toward the open bar."

I bit my tongue before I pointed out the irony in his comment, silently willing the servers to avoid Uncle Albert's grabby hands before he choked on an appetizer.

Just when I wondered how much longer I'd have to endure the man's company solo, I caught sight of Lothian. He arrived looking strikingly handsome in a tailored suit, his crisp lavender shirt contrasted perfectly against his artfully styled hair.

"Astra, there you are! I wondered where my favorite maid of honor had wandered off to." Lothian gave me a quick once-over as if to assure

I was still in one piece. "And who might this gentleman be?"

I glared.

Of course, he'd come to check on me.

The werewolf made it his personal mission to mysteriously turn up wherever I went, usually right when I didn't need or want his hovering.

Uncle Albert's whole demeanor changed in an instant once he spotted Lothian. His formerly drooping mustache twitched with delight as he reached out to eagerly shake the werewolf's hand. "Lothian, m'boy! I've heard so much about you. Made quite a name for yourself in business, I understand?"

Lothian chuckled, turning on the charm to greet Uncle Albert. "I do try my best, sir. And you are...?"

"This is Albert Sullivan, Emma's uncle," I said.

"Wonderful to meet you." Lothian gave Uncle Albert a conspiratorial wink. "I have to say, anyone related to the lovely Emma is a friend of mine."

The fat man's cheeks were rosy with pleasure. "Oh, ho! The pleasure's all mine, son! All mine! Wonderful to meet you! Just wonderful! Heard you've got investments up and down the whole coast. Gladder than ever now our Emma's marrying into your pack."

Lothian blinked at the word "pack," momentarily caught off guard, and the muscles around his jaw tightened.

I could understand his reaction. Very few knew that there were paranormals at the wedding, and it was implausible anyone had told this bumbling fool that Emma's betrothed, Eddie, was the head of a werewolf pack. Uncle Albert probably didn't mean "pack" in the strictest sense of the word.

And yet, it made me uneasy—and clearly surprised Lothian.

The werewolf covered deftly, however, by arching an eyebrow and allowing the hint of a smirk to play at the corner of his mouth. "We're quite fond of your niece, sir, and are very happy to have her. Emma's made Eddie very happy."

"Yes, yes, good for people to be happy." Uncle Albert dabbed at the perspiration beading on his forehead with a napkin, his usually ruddy complexion looking paler than before. "Warm in here tonight, don't you think? Or is it just me?"

The club felt like it was air-conditioned on a subzero setting, so it was definitely just him.

His digestive system was probably overheating.

"Are you feeling all right, sir?" Lothian asked, a note of concern in his voice.

Uncle Albert waved away his question with an impatient flap of his hand. "Fine, fine. Probably just one too many of these bacon treats. I have to watch my cholesterol, you know. That's why I'm only eating the ones with the vegetables."

Just then, a thin, dark-haired woman in her late twenties stormed into the club, eyes blazing with rage. She scanned the room from the top of the stairs and spotted Uncle Albert at our table. Without skipping a beat, she raced down the stairs, marched right up to him, and hissed through gritted teeth, "There you are! I've been looking everywhere for you. Trying to avoid me?"

"What do you want, Beatrice?" Uncle Albert asked, almost meekly recoiling back. "Can't you see I'm in the middle of a conversation with Emma's lovely friends?"

So this was the notorious niece he'd been complaining about earlier. Her eyes were narrow, and her fists were clenched at her sides as if she were just waiting to let loose on her uncle.

"Don't give me that, Uncle! You know exactly why I'm here." Beatrice jabbed a finger at his belly as she scolded through gritted teeth. "We need to talk. Now."

Lothian took the cue and offered Beatrice his most charming smile. "It was lovely chatting, but we should let you two have some privacy. Come, Astra." He placed a guiding hand on my back, and I ignored the urge to turn, put him in a wrist lock, and flip him.

He was the best man, after all. Emma might be upset.

As we walked away, I overheard Beatrice hiss, "You're not going to get away with cutting me out! I deserve what you promised!" Uncle Albert's response faded into the noise of clinking glasses and chatter filling the club.

LOTHIAN GUIDED me to a corner where Rex, Emma's vampire brother, was surrounded by two flirtatious young women. As we approached, he flashed them his signature vampire grin and smoothly bowed out of the conversation, standing at attention as soon as his eyes met Lothian's.

"Thanks for giving me an excuse to bow out of that. Everything going well so far?" Rex asked us as he gestured toward the club dotted with pink frills and ribbons that clashed with his usual taste for gothic decor. "She wanted pink."

"Emma seems happy, and that's all that matters to Eddie," Lothian said. "I think some family drama might be starting early, though. Reunions can be trying, especially when there's an open bar involved."

Rex grimaced. "You don't have to tell me twice. I've already had Aunt Mildred pinching my cheeks and lamenting how 'peaked' I'm looking these days. She told me to get more sun." He rolled his eyes. "That woman could make a corpse feel conscious about its pallor."

We laughed.

Emma's vampire brother tucked his hands into his pockets with a rueful shake of his head. "At least cousin Beatrice complimented my 'gothic hotness' and said it was a shame we were related. Small oddities of dealing with my human family, I suppose."

At the mention of Beatrice, my curiosity flared.

"Do you know Beatrice well? I was just talking to your Uncle Albert, and she came over. She seemed furious." When Rex didn't start spilling the tea, I added, "I was wondering what it was all about."

"At its core? Bea and Uncle Albert have never seen eye to eye." Rex shrugged. "She's always been the black sheep, while he doted on Emma as the golden niece. Now that Albert's getting on in years, I think Bea's afraid he'll cut her out of the will in favor of leaving everything to his business partner or Emma. Aunt Mildred claims they argue over it constantly."

"Money does strange things to people," Lothian mused. "Turns caring family members into vultures at the first scent of an inheritance."

"It's ironic, of course—Emma doesn't need his money at all, but no one knows she's marrying into a werewolf empire." Rex grimaced, flashing a hint of fang. "I tried to warn Uncle Albert and Bea that family occasions like weddings are a breeding ground for drama. But they both insisted on coming, and that they would behave, so here we are. Bea will likely cause a scene, Albert's blood pressure will skyrocket, and I'll be left playing referee. As usual."

A slight curl of the corner of Lothian's lip betrayed his amusement. "Sounds like fun," he said to Rex.

"Does it?"

"No. No, it does not."

"Remind me again why I offered to organize all this?"

Lothian clapped him on the back with a sympathetic smile. "Because you're a good brother. The night's still young—maybe the drama has already peaked?"

I doubted it.

"Rex, you've done an amazing job translating Emma's absolutely lunatic level of girly into reality. That's why you offered. And the catering staff you hired have certainly outdone themselves"—I held up a Cucumber Cup with Herbed Cream Cheese and Smoked Salmon —"not that your uncle has left much for the other guests."

Rex followed my pointed look to where Uncle Albert was waylaying yet another server, his plate piled high with various hors d'oeuvres.

"He really shouldn't be eating those," Rex said as his uncle grabbed fried chicken wings with both chubby hands. "My dad says Uncle Albert has high blood pressure, high cholesterol, diabetes, and on top of all that, the man smokes cigarettes and cigars. Honestly, sometimes I wonder how he's lived this long."

"Some people are tough to kill," Lothian said.

While the two of them began chatting about immortality, my attention wandered over the sea of mingling wedding guests.

Uncle Albert and Beatrice continued their argument in a far corner as the chubby man chomped on his chicken wings, their hands gesturing aggressively. Though attempting discretion, their body language radiated anger.

My brow furrowed in concern as Uncle Albert suddenly wiped at his brow and leaned against a nearby wall for support. I was quite a distance from him, but I could tell he seemed short of breath, shaking off Beatrice's attempts to... steady him?

"Uncle Albert looks like he doesn't seem to be feeling well. I'm going to go check on him," I said, already moving away from Rex and Lothian and in Uncle Albert's direction. By the time I reached the corner, Uncle Albert's complexion had taken on a sickly pallor under the sparkling chandeliers' warm glow.

"Uncle Albert, are you feeling all right?"

"He's fine," Beatrice snapped. "Mind your own business."

I stepped closer and called his name.

Albert jolted, his body going rigid as he stared at me with widened eyes. His pupils were dilated, and his mouth opened and closed like a goldfish gasping for air. "I'm not...not quite myself, I don't think. But thank you for asking." He blinked sluggishly before turning back to Beatrice. "Now see here, you vulture, I won't be badgered into changing my will on the weekend of a family wedding. Whatever I've done I had to do, and you'll be taken care of. Now just stop this nonsense. This behavior is not decent."

"How dare you talk about decency after what you've done! I'm looking out for myself, as I've always had to do!" Beatrice shot back, cheeks flushed in anger and embarrassment at being caught arguing again. "I knew you'd be like this. You never cared for me after Mom died, so why start now?"

Lothian materialized at my side, surveying the scene with a frown. "Is there a problem here?"

Man, he was annoying.

However, Lothian's interruption gave Beatrice pause, and a guarded look passed between the feuding relatives.

Uncle Albert drew himself up, mustering as much dignity as possible while still unsteady. "No problem at all. My niece and I were just...reminiscing. Weren't we, Beatrice?"

Beatrice's eyes narrowed at her uncle's blatant

attempt to save face. "Yes. Reminiscing." With that said, she spun on her heel and stalked off into the crowd.

Uncle Albert sagged against the wall with a weary sigh. I placed a hand on his arm, concerned by the clammy feel of his skin. "Are you certain you're all right, Uncle Albert? You don't look well."

He patted my hand in a paternal fashion, offering a wan smile. "Quite certain, my dear. Weddings and family, you know...the stress is enough to make any man feel under the weather." But something in Uncle Albert's glassy gaze told me his indisposition might run deeper than that.

I watched, concerned, as Uncle Albert walked away.

\* \* \*

A BLOND BLUR rocketed across the room, sparkly shoes flashing as she flew at me with her arms outstretched. I was enveloped in a cloud of joy and a flurry of tulle and lace when she reached me. "There's my maid of honor! I was hoping I'd run into you."

Eddie appeared at Emma's side within seconds, amusement glinting in his eyes as he watched his bride-to-be embrace me. It amused me that my friend's happiness was mirrored in the alpha werewolf's face, and it seemed like almost-wedded bliss had created an extra glow about the pair.

"Where's the world's tiniest ring bearer?" I asked.

Emma waved away my question, unconcerned. "With my parents. Honestly, I don't think they plan on giving Hunter back until well after the honeymoon at this point." Her laughter held a note of relief. "He's in good hands. Tell me truthfully, how do you think everything's going so far?" She blinked. "It's not too pink, is it?"

It was too pink.

Everything was too pink.

Not that I would ever say that to Emma's face. Or, honestly, behind her back. Her voluminous tulle gown had a high probability of concealing any number of possible weapons.

Before I could answer, a curvy brunette with curly dark hair and bright blue eyes spun toward us in a flurry of swirling red silk, her arms outstretched for an enthusiastic embrace. "Emma, this is all so exciting! You look absolutely gorgeous."

Emma opened her arms, a bewildered look on

her face.

The woman's gaze swept over Emma's gown and Eddie with unconcealed delight. "Vincent and I are having a wonderful time. Everyone's having a wonderful time! Well, not everyone." She tilted her head, her eyes narrowing a bit. "I have to admit, your Uncle Albert seemed a bit off earlier. Is everything all right?"

Emma blinked in confusion. "Oh my gosh. Cousin Connie? Is that you?"

"Of course it's me!" The brunette laughed with a warm, rich sound and waved away Emma's question. "Who else would it be?"

A flicker of bafflement crossed Emma's face, turning her usually savvy expression into one of puzzled befuddlement. "Who else would it be?" Emma echoed. "Your hair used to be blond, and you have to be a hundred pounds lighter. Honestly, Connie, you look amazing!"

"Right, yes, I realize that. I do. I don't know why dishwater blond is even a color. God should have sent that down to hell with the devil. That's what He should have done." Connie flushed, tucking a loose curl behind her ear. "Not that I would ever tell God what he should do."

A shadowy figure materialized behind Connie, a man whose voice had the timbre of a cello being strummed. "Connie," he uttered in a low drawl, the single word holding a tone of deep-rooted familiarity, "I'll go check on Albert."

"Right, yes, thanks, Vincent!"

"Who's he?" Emma looked confused again. "Do I know him? Are we related?"

"No, he's my date, silly! Vincent De Luca? The Midnight Hour?"

Emma just looked at her blankly.

"It's a talk show on KBOO 98.3? Really? You've never heard of it?"

"Sure, Emma, you know the one," Lothian said, leaning in. "Vincent chats with callers about all sorts of conspiracy theories. UFOs, vampires, werewolves. Lots of unsolved mystery type stuff." He looked at me pointedly.

Well.

That didn't seem good.

"Yes!" Connie said. "Yes, that's him! Are you a fan?"

The werewolf responded, "Huge fan," his words heavily soaked in a sarcasm.

With her eyebrows arching into sharp crescents of suspicion, Emma posed her next question with the rising tenacity of a detective on a cold case. "Hold on a minute, why exactly is Vincent checking on my Uncle Albert?"

"Vincent knows your uncle." Connie waited and added, "You did know your Uncle Albert owns the radio station, right? We were chatting, and Vincent mentioned your uncle seemed a bit pale during their conversation. I just wanted to check in with you guys to see if he was okay. Since I'm a nurse, I thought I could help." She shrugged apologetically. "Maybe I should have just gone to find your Mom. You must be busy with all the wedding stuff."

Curiosity was slowly taking over Emma's face, like a vine finding its way up a brick wall.

Curiosity Eddie was not about to let derail this wedding.

"Pleasure to meet you, Connie. I'm Eddie, Emma's fiancé." His smile exuded charm and welcome. "I appreciate your concern for Emma's uncle, but I just spoke to him and he's doing just fine as far as I know. Likely just the excitement of the evening." He gave Emma's hand a reassuring squeeze. "Nothing to look into here, am I right, Emma?"

Emma did not answer him, but he looked relieved as Connie launched enthusiastically into wedding details and asked Emma question after question about the couple's future plans.

# CHAPTER THREE

*N*o sooner had Emma and the vivacious cousin Connie wandered off amid laughter and wedding chatter than Lothian appeared at my side. "A word, if you don't mind?"

I barely suppressed a groan, steeling my gaze as I rotated to view him. "What is it this time? We've done our walk down the aisle thing. We know where we're supposed to stand. What could you possibly need now?"

With an amused glare, he guided me to a secluded corner and leaned in close (I assumed) to avoid being overheard. "Astra, Eddie charged me with ensuring nothing disrupted Emma's wedding weekend. I have to ask—are you deliberately stirring up drama with that Uncle Albert business?"

"You're seriously offensive, you know that?" My eyes narrowed at the implication. "I'm not 'stirring up' anything. There's history between Albert and Beatrice, and that history is boiling over whether I dig into it or not. I want the same thing you do, dog—for Emma's fluffy pink Barbie Dream wedding not to implode."

"I'm not trying to accuse you of anything, Astra, but I feel like we have enough complications without hunting for more." Lothian's jaw tightened. "For instance, this Vincent De Luca character. Do you have any idea the kind of crackpot that man is?"

"I don't make it a habit to listen to talk radio in the middle of the night, no."

"De Luca is a vocal 'occult expert' who spends half his airtime railing against the existence of anything supernatural and the other half sermonizing and demonizing what he believes exists. Werewolves, vampires, witches are all figments of overactive imaginations or demons sent from hell."

"And he's dating cousin Connie. That can't be a coincidence."

"Remember, Astra—whatever paranormal

beings might be in this room, they're unknown to many." Lothian glanced over toward Connie. "Emma's police work with you is known. And your psychometry power? The Forkbridge paper has written about it multiple times."

I nodded. The last thing we needed was some self-proclaimed "occult expert" sniffing around. "What do you think he's here for?"

Lothian's eyes shifted around the room, not settling on any one thing but instead skimming with concern. "No idea. Go shake his hand."

"Well, aren't you a comedian? He won't let me near him if he knows who I am."

"You're probably right. You've been a topic of his show more than once."

My surprise was instantaneous, and I jerked my head back to look at Lothian. "I've been what now?"

Lothian's eyes were sharp and focused, searching my face for some indication of what I was thinking. "De Luca has devoted followers who call in insisting they've seen proof of monsters in their midst. He eggs them on and stirs up fear and paranoia. The man is unhinged —and now here he is, cozying up to Emma's cousin?" He shook his head. "I don't like it one bit. Whatever is going on between Beatrice and

Albert isn't as important as De Luca showing up here."

"Do you think he knows about..." I let the implication hang, uncertain of saying too much even in this secluded spot, but the memory of Uncle Albert's words lingered in my mind. His use of the word pack in a way that seemed almost deliberate.

"There's no way to know if he suspects the truth. But men like De Luca always search for ways to validate their delusions. The possibility he might stumble onto real evidence this weekend is troubling." Lothian ran a hand through his hair, sighing. "Rex and I will watch him and try to divert his attention elsewhere. I just need you to promise you won't start a private investigation that might attract Emma's notice. She's got enough stress as it is."

"Rex knows?" I asked.

Lothian pointed across the room where the vampire was watching us. Stupid vampire super hearing. Totally overrated, too, if you ask me. Seriously, who needs to hear a pin drop from three blocks away?

Lothian's eyes searched mine, silently willing me to agree.

I knew if it were up to him, Emma'd be

wrapped in protective spells, padding, and ignorance until well after the honeymoon. But avoiding drama wasn't so simple when trouble had a way of finding all of us without any of us trying very hard.

But...

The last thing I wanted was to add another wrinkle to Emma's worry lines or cast a cloud over her day. She deserved to bask in the glow of her special moment. Well, figuratively speaking, of course. Owing to her brother's sun-allergic vampiric condition, the celebrations were slated to begin once the Florida sun slipped below the horizon.

The whole affair was more moonlit soiree than a sun-kissed garden party.

But it was very pink.

"All right, I'll do my best to steer Emma clear of mystery and mayhem as much as possible. But you know if something happens, I can't guarantee anything!"

The hint of a smile played at the corner of Lothian's mouth. "Fair enough. Just remember— no hunting for clues that don't need to be hunted or stirring pots that don't need to be stirred. Besides, I'll need your help keeping an eye on De Luca."

With that, Lothian slipped back into the crowd, leaving me to wonder just how much chaos might erupt without my so-called 'help.' When it came to Emma's wedding, trouble didn't need an invitation, and avoiding it entirely might prove impossible.

I wished Archie was here. His sarcastic running commentary always made events like this more amusing. But for the sake of appearances, Emma had insisted that my sisters and I leave our familiars at home for the wedding weekend. She didn't want any eerily clever companions raising eyebrows, and I understood her point.

Her vampire brother was going to be tough enough to explain.

We'd all made sacrifices to grant Emma her perfect human fantasy wedding and a few days of blissful mundane normality, and nothing was going to ruin her pink-spun sugar dream of a wedding if I had any say in the matter.

* * *

THE CHATTER and clink of glasses faded into background noise as I circulated through the crowd.

When I spotted Uncle Albert's familiar rotund figure across the room, he was once again piling a plate high at one of the buffet stations, sampling delicacies with abandon. I winced, wishing the obese man would heed warnings to slow down, but I knew enough to realize any protest on my part (or anyone else's) would fall on deaf ears. Uncle Albert appeared to be the type of man determined to indulge. Consequences be damned.

And those consequences seemed to be creeping ever closer.

Even from a distance, I could see his hands trembling, face flushed from more than just the room's warmth. A strange feeling of foreboding washed over me, brows knitting with worry. I started weaving through guests to make my way over, hoping I was wrong. I just wanted to grab Albert's hand and use my power to make sure he was all right.

Before I could reach Uncle Albert, he froze—and panic lit his features. His mouth opened and closed uselessly as he clutched at his throat, struggling to draw breath. The realization hit me like a physical blow—he was choking.

"Someone help him!" My cry rang out as I broke into a run, stupid high heels be damned.

But a crowd had already gathered around Uncle Albert, pounding him on the back to no avail. His face turned from red to purple, eyes bulging in terror as he fought for air in vain.

Chaos erupted through the room, guests shouting for medics and crying in alarm.

Within seconds, Lothian had materialized and shoved through the crowd. He surveyed the scene and cursed under his breath. Positioning himself behind Uncle Albert, Lothian wrapped his arms around the obese man's torso and jerked upward with practiced precision.

A chunk of half-chewed food dislodged from Albert's throat and arced across the room, eliciting gasps of horror. But Uncle Albert remained motionless, face still tinted blue, eyes glassy and unseeing. Lothian swore and lowered Albert to the floor, checking for any signs of life or breath to no avail.

"I don't understand," I whispered. "It wasn't that long. He should be breathing."

Lothian leaned back on his heels; the werewolf's gaze met mine. His grim expression said it all—he sensed the damage was already done.

Uncle Albert's fate was now out of anyone's hands.

My knees went weak, and I had a hollow feeling in my chest as Emma rushed to her uncle's side. Her tear-streaked face turned to Lothian in disbelief. All I could do was watch from a distance as my helplessness and dread sank in, replaying those final moments over in a futile attempt to determine what should have been done differently.

I moved through the crowd and leaned across from Lothian, touching Uncle Albert's still-warm hand. My psychometry power surged as images flooded my mind... I saw the buffet table through Uncle Albert's eyes, felt the excitement at so many delicacies left to sample. There was a strange breathlessness, a tightness in his chest, but he ignored it, too eager to fill his plate.

Then I felt his throat closing up around a bite of mini-quiche, panic rising as he struggled to draw breath or call out. He clutched at his throat helplessly, each failed attempt at inhaling like a knife to the lungs, terror flooding his system. He grabbed a piece of steak and swallowed, thinking it would dislodge whatever was stuck.

It didn't.

Faces swam into view, blurred by tears as the burning need for oxygen grew more desperate. His heartbeat thundered in my ears, the pulse of it slowing. The edges of the vision darkened, closing in as all other sensations drifted away into nothingness.

Strong hands grasped my shoulders, giving me a shake. "Astra! What did you see?"

Lothian.

I swallowed hard and opened my eyes, meeting his worried gaze. There was no lying or downplaying what I'd witnessed. "The quiche was blocking, and he couldn't breathe, and then everything slowed down, went black..."

I could see it in the judgmental faces staring down at the fat man. See their thoughts written on their faces. Uncle Albert had sealed his fate through sheer stubbornness and denial, unwilling to accept his limitations or spare a thought for moderation or consequences. It was sad he died, yes. A terrible tragedy. But clearly not a surprise.

Rex appeared in a flourish of inhuman speed, taking in the scene with widening eyes. "I called 911. Is he—"

The question hung in the air.

Several other guests were openly sobbing now, while others looked on in stunned and horrified silence. The boisterous celebration ground to an awkward halt.

"He's gone," Lothian told the vampire, even

though he knew that Rex could sense that Albert's heart no longer beat.

The vampire's shoulders slumped in defeat as he moved to take his weeping sister into his arms, offering what comfort he could as Eddie and Lothian covered Uncle Albert with a tablecloth.

* * *

A HUSH FELL over the club as the paramedics wheeled Uncle Albert's shrouded form through the crowd toward the exit. Only the click of cameras and murmur of grim speculation broke the silence, a macabre fascination with misfortune and drama that lent a surreal quality to the moment.

"That's really gross," I muttered as a guest I didn't know snapped the last photo.

Lothian stood at my side, his gaze fixed on Vincent De Luca across the room. The radio host's eyes followed Uncle Albert's progress, an unreadable expression on his face. Certainly not the shock or dismay one might expect.

"He doesn't seem particularly upset, does he?" Lothian murmured.

"Are you looking for suspicious activity now? After the lecture you gave me?"

"I told you I thought he was our primary problem." Lothian shrugged, though his stare remained trained on De Luca. "But look—even Beatrice hasn't shed a single tear over her dear uncle's demise. One might think she'd be distraught after their argument earlier."

He had a point.

Lothian and I scanned the guests, noting their expressions and demeanor. Most looked properly shocked, horrified, or saddened by the grim turn of events.

But not all.

Beatrice leaned against a nearby wall, arms crossed, surveying the scene with a veiled look of annoyance rather than grief. Her gaze lacked the glassy sheen of unshed tears or any trace of sorrow, fixed instead on Uncle Albert's retreating form as if it were an inconvenience now resolved.

"That is weird, actually," I admitted. "I heard her yell at Albert about changing his will. Or maybe he yelled at her that he wouldn't change his will. Either way, it implies that she wanted him to change it. If she did and he died before doing it, wouldn't she be more upset?"

"Okay, but De Luca has fresh fodder for his radio show, warning listeners about the Sullivan's and Emma's wedding being cursed or whatever he'll make up about a choking death by an overweight man."

Vincent De Luca watched the proceedings as well, a fox among hapless hens, his keen-eyed interest setting him apart. There was a glint of something calculating and avid in that gaze, wheels already turning behind it as if he was watching some macabre future segment unfold. The radio host's lips curved not into a frown but something closer to a smirk of satisfaction, an expression jarringly out of place.

Lothian's jaw tightened. "I don't like it, Astra."

"So, about that choking-to-death thing?"

"Yes?"

"I'm not sure he choked."

The remaining guests had descended into clusters of hushed speculation, a voyeuristic need to dissect tragedy that lent a surreal quality to the aftermath. Their tones held notes of grim fascination rather than genuine empathy, as quick to judge the dead man's appetite and habit of excess as mourn the loss.

I lowered my voice, leaning in close to Lothian. "When I touched Uncle Albert earlier, what I sensed—it wasn't him choking on steak."

Lothian's eyebrows rose. "What do you mean?"

"I felt his throat start to close up when he ate the mini-quiche, not the steak. Panic, struggling to breathe. But when you performed the Heimlich, the only thing that came up was a chunk of steak." I shrugged. "Do people usually choke on quiche?"

"No idea, but it wouldn't seem so. You can choke on anything if the circumstances are right, but I don't know. I'm not a doctor." Lothian's eyes narrowed, mind working to put the pieces together. "You think his reaction was due to an allergy?"

"Possibly. We know he had health issues, and allergies often come along with those. The quiche could've triggered anaphylaxis if he was allergic to something in it."

I bit my lip, uncertain how much speculation was too much. But if there was any chance Uncle Albert's death was not natural causes, we needed to determine it now before the trail went cold.

Lothian seemed to read my thoughts, his voice dropping to a hushed murmur. "You suspect foul play."

It was not phrased as a question. I gave the barest nod, continuing in the same discreet tone. "The timeline doesn't match what I sensed, and his symptoms seem too severe, too fast, for a simple choking. I could be mistaken, but..."

"But it's enough to warrant a discreet investigation." Lothian sighed, running a hand through his hair. "Emma will want answers, even if we have to shield her from the worst possibilities."

"If someone wanted Uncle Albert out of the way, his poor health and habits made the perfect smokescreen. His death might appear to be natural causes to anyone not looking too closely." My chest constricted at the thought, anger bubbling beneath the surface. To use a wedding as a cover for murder, disrupting joy for selfish gain...it was unconscionable.

And yet if my hunch proved right, that might be exactly what we were dealing with.

# CHAPTER FOUR

With the paramedics gone and Uncle Albert's body removed from the premises, an awkward atmosphere descended over Emma's rehearsal dinner. The guests had broken into hushed clusters, rehashing the grim events in shocked tones. Lothian and I stood to the side watching the various reactions and conversations unfold.

Eventually, my sisters made their way over to where we were stationed.

Althea, ever the practical one, peered around the room with a critical eye. "Quite the damper on the festivities. Do you think the wedding will still go on as scheduled?"

Before I could respond, Ami stepped closer

and lowered her voice. "I think so, but something's off here. I'm getting strange vibes." She turned to me. "You touched Albert as he left this plane. You must have seen something, yes?"

I nodded. "When I touched him, the visions I got didn't match up with choking on food. At least I don't think they did. He started choking before swallowing the steak, which felt like an allergic reaction." I explained to them what I had sensed and my conversation with Lothian.

Ami's brows furrowed. "An anaphylaxis allergic reaction could have happened that fast— but you said you think it happened after he ate the quiche. Right?" Her brows furrowed, and her lips tightened as she squinted, unsure what to make of the situation. "I saw him eating it earlier, and there was no reaction."

"Could he have an anaphylaxis reaction later? Like an hour later?" I asked.

"No," Althea said. "Well, let me clarify. The anaphylactic shock from an allergen can come on quickly, but it's not usually instantaneous. In rare cases, anaphylaxis may be delayed for hours, but he probably would have had indications. Hives, itching. Flushed or pale skin."

"He didn't look well," I pointed out.

"Yeah, but he had a lot of medical issues. And

if he was allergic to something that would hit him that fast, wouldn't he have an EpiPen on him?" Lothian asked. "He wasn't reaching for one."

"You didn't check for one, though, because you thought he was choking," Ami told the werewolf. "He might have had one."

Althea's forehead creased, and her eyebrows drew together. "Ingredients in quiche like eggs, cheese, and shellfish are common allergens, but I feel like if he was that allergic to something in that quiche—which appeared to contain pretty common ingredients—Albert would know." Althea paused, then added, "And he had far more than a single bite." She gestured toward the table. "Add that to the lack of an EpiPen, which could have possibly reversed the anaphylaxis if caught quickly enough... I don't know. The whole thing just seems off."

"Okay. Foul play hasn't been ruled out." I turned to Lothian. "Tell them about Vincent De Luca and Beatrice's behavior."

Lothian described De Luca's calculated interest in the paranormal and Beatrice's marked lack of grief over her estranged uncle's death. "I think there are enough questionable details and suspicious behavior to warrant discreetly—very discreetly—investigating further."

I turned to Ayla, our resident ghost whisperer. "Did you see Uncle Albert's spirit after he passed? Is he still here, maybe?"

Ayla nodded, a perplexed look on her face. "I did see him, but only for a moment. Right after he died, his ghost came bursting out of his body and disappeared through the front wall like his tail was on fire. Honestly, I've never seen a spirit move on that quickly. Usually, they linger for at least a short time, curious about their whole death scene thing, but Uncle Albert fled as fast as he could go."

"Huh." Lothian rubbed his chin in thought. "What could make a ghost run away from a bunch of mortals? No one here can do anything to him, right?"

No one had an answer as my mind spun with theories and unanswered questions.

"One thing I know for sure. Okay, well, not for sure. But mostly for sure." I looked between my sisters and Lothian. "Uncle Albert's death was no accident. I just can't see someone choking on quiche. Honestly."

"You realize that's kind of a flimsy foundation, right?" Althea asked.

"I don't know that she's right about that, Thea, but there's something off about what happened here tonight," Ami said, her hand in her pocket. "I can feel it."

A somber mood fell over our group as we stood sure that something happened, but with no evidence that it did. If there was a killer, there was a good chance they hid in plain sight among the wedding guests—possibly ready to strike again if it served their sinister purpose for all we knew.

Ami glanced around, her expression worried. "Do you really think Emma will go through with the wedding after this?"

Before I could respond, Rex appeared by our side in a flourish of preternatural speed. Vampires certainly had a talent for sneaking up on people. "Emma's determined to proceed as planned. She wants to 'honor' Uncle Albert's memory rather than let his passing cast a gloom over her special day."

I arched a brow at the vampire. "No offense meant here, but Uncle Albert didn't seem particularly cherished. The only time I saw him talking to any of your family, he and Beatrice were yelling at each other."

"You're not wrong." Rex's thin lips pressed together as one corner of his mouth turned upward in a faint gesture of distaste. "Albert was loved in the obligatory sense that he was family, but I don't think anyone would call him well-liked."

"Why's that?" I asked.

If Uncle Albert's unpleasant nature earned him more enemies than friends, it gave a further motive for foul play.

The vampire thought for a moment, then shrugged. "He was rude, arrogant, and cared only for himself. He felt entitled to all of the Sullivan family money—which wasn't much—and made no secret that he thought my grandfather should have left him the bulk of the inheritance and cut out my father. Any gathering Albert attended inevitably ended in quarrel over money or perceived slights."

I looked at him, surprised. "I didn't think your family was wealthy, Rex."

"I told you, it wasn't much, but what there was my father gave Albert rather than fight with him."

Ami's mouth was wide open, her lips parted in shock. "Why would he do that?"

The vampire typically had a face of stone, with a stern expression and a sharp jawline. But when Rex cracked a tiny half-smile, the corners of his lips curved up ever so slightly, and his dark eyes twinkled. "That's who my dad is. Family comes first." The stone face returned. "Gratitude for that, though, was not who Albert was. It didn't help."

Rex related a few instances of Albert causing scenes at family events, teasing his brother for being a "dumb jock" or not being as monetarily successful, his sense of self-importance and greed making him an unpleasant addition to any occasion. The more I learned of the man's reprehensible behavior, the less surprised I was at the possibility someone may have offed the guy.

I was a little annoyed, though, that they'd done it at Emma's wedding.

* * *

THE PARTY slowly recovered from the shock of Albert's unexpected death. Drinks started to flow again, and chatter picked back up. Given enough time, people will grasp at any semblance of normalcy and comfort and head toward it like a moth toward a flame. No one attends a wedding hoping for a funeral, after all.

The guests seemed determined to salvage what remained of the evening, and the morbid fascination with Albert's demise had worn off. Overheard discussions shifted to lighter topics, nostalgic stories of the bride and groom, and family memories. Laughter rang out here and there.

Like a seasoned captain smoothly navigating choppy waters, Emma wove her way through the bustling room, playing the part of the unflappable hostess. She stopped to exchange words with friends and family, her voice a soft murmur blending into the ambient hum of the gathering.

Amid the hellos and how are you's, her eyes darted covertly toward the exit as if Uncle Albert's ghost might reappear at any moment.

Not that she would know it.

Eddie remained faithfully by Emma's side, his watchful eye following his fiancé's every move. He looked ready to whisk her away from the festivities at the first sign of her composure crumbling or the disaster overwhelming her.

There was no need.

Emma soldiered on, determined to face each guest out of a sense of duty (as well as a desire to exert her sheer will against the gloom to get the pink wedding back on track.)

As I watched her, Lothian reappeared at my side. "Did you uncover anything new while mingling?"

"I didn't mingle. But no, nothing groundbreaking in the last ten minutes."

"My apologies." Lothian flashed a roguish grin. "I sometimes forget your talents aren't always active. A beautiful woman like you, I tend to get distracted."

I rolled my eyes at his flirtatious remark.

So far, he'd been behaving—no flirting, no comments that hinted at more, no compliments that made me want to punch him in the face. I couldn't deny the werewolf was attractive, but his cocksure attitude had grated on me since the first day I met him.

I gestured across the room toward Ami, conversing with Beatrice, and Althea chatted with a serious-looking Vincent De Luca. "My sisters seem to be working the room. Maybe they found something."

Ayla stood by the buffet, carefully surveying the remaining food selections as she spoke quietly with one of the catering staff. I had no doubt she was inquiring about quiche ingredients and possibly food handling procedures.

Lothian followed my gaze, his expression sobering as he watched my sisters discreetly investigating. His cheeky attitude quickly disappeared. "I know they're smart, your sisters.

But do they understand how dangerous poking around a potential murder might be?"

"We've investigated murders together before. They know to tread carefully."

A frown creased Lothian's brow. "I still don't like you all putting yourself in danger. This is our responsibility, not yours. That and your power can leave you vulnerable when touching objects or people directly linked to violent events, right?"

I bit the inside of my cheek and crossed my arms over my chest as I slowly exhaled. I was not in the mood for Lothian Pennington's misplaced chivalry. He didn't know me well enough to offer opinions on my powers or capabilities. "I don't believe I asked for your permission or approval. This is what I do—what my sisters and I do together. Normally, it's what Emma and I do, but she's busy this weekend."

A flicker of annoyance passed over Lothian's features, his jaw tightening at my sharp retort. But the werewolf exhaled a resigned sigh, conceding the point. "You are one of the most stubborn women I've ever met. I'm not trying to say you're less capable without Emma. I am saying that having a partner... well, there's a reason they tend to recommend that. It's just safer with two pairs of experienced eyes."

"Are you offering?"

"I thought I was being clear that I was."

"Don't need one. I'll be sure to holler if I require rescuing, though."

Lothian shook his head, calling me stubborn once more. "Look, I'm only trying to follow Eddie's orders—make sure no drama ruins Emma's perfect wedding weekend. But if you don't want to team up, fine. Besides..." He reached into his pocket and pulled out a hotel key card, dangling it in front of me. "Only one of us has Albert's hotel room key card, and it's not you. So I think I can handle this better, anyway."

* * *

MY EYES WIDENED at the sight of the hotel key card.

How on earth did Lothian get his hands on that?

I peered around to ensure no one was close enough to overhear before hissing in a low voice, "Did you steal from a corpse? Seriously?"

"No. I did not. No one thinks he was murdered." The werewolf shrugged. "I just asked for it, the paramedics gave it to me, and I volunteered to take care of his personal effects, checking him out of the hotel, and all that stuff they prefer not to be bothered with. I'm very charming, you know."

"I disagree."

"No, you don't. Anyway, since you're not interested..." He started to slip the card back into his pocket.

"Give me that!" I tried to snatch it from his hand, but my fingers only grazed the card as he yanked it out of my reach. My fingers tingled where I'd brushed it, my power surging as glimpses of Albert's life flooded my mind.

Uncle Albert entering his room, dropping his wallet and key card on the desk. Housekeeping staff cleaning and tidying, unaware of the drama about to unfold.

Lothian slipped it back into his pocket with a smirk.

"You really are a jerk. Thief."

Lothian arched a brow, his expression mildly offended. "I didn't steal anything. I was given the key and will use it to aid in the discreet investigation. As discussed." He leaned forward and lowered his voice to almost a whisper. "Do you really think Emma wants the police traipsing through Albert's room, scrutinizing his potential secrets and possibly airing family or paranormal laundry to her coworkers? That crack about a pack may have meant nothing. But it may have meant something."

I pinched the bridge of my nose, exhaling another frustrated sigh.

As much as I hated to admit it, Lothian had a point.

Conducting our own covert search of Albert's room before authorities descended (if they ever descended—because Lothian was also right in that no one official thought he might have been murdered) might uncover clues and spare Emma discomfort.

"Emma knows I have the hotel key, Astra," Lothian pressed, reading my wavering resolve. "If you want, I can get the pack to stand guard to ensure no one disturbs us. If we find anything useful, we'll share it with the police. But at least this way, we dictate how and what comes to light —just in case this has anything to do with things we'd all rather remain under wraps."

I met Lothian's expectant gaze, his jaw set with determination. "Fine. But we do this quickly and carefully. In and out, minimal disruption." I gestured toward the pocketed key card with a shake of my head. "Honestly, Pennington, you have all the subtlety of a battering ram."

The werewolf's eyes glinted with mischief and triumph, apparently choosing to overlook my criticism in light of gaining my compliance. "Subtlety is overrated. I may sometimes be a battering ram, but I'm an expedient and efficient battering ram. That's why Eddie keeps me around. Well, that and my sparkling personality." Lothian scanned the clusters of guests and lowered his voice. "Let's slip away now while people's attention is still occupied by the open bar."

I nodded, wordlessly turning to follow Lothian toward the exit. We had barely taken two steps when I heard the unmistakable click of heels against the marble floor advancing toward us with haste.

Emma's floral perfume wafted ahead before she'd made her presence known.

Her pink chiffon dress fluttered around her as she stopped right in front of us and crossed her arms. Her keen eyes bounced back and forth as if trying to unravel some mystery, her brows furrowing with suspicion. "Where are you two sneaking off to?"

Lothian flashed her an easy grin. "My apologies, Emma. Astra finally agreed to have that drink with me in private. I wasn't going to pass up the opportunity."

Oh, he did not just do that.

But he did.

He absolutely did.

I tensely clenched my jaw, plastered a thin smile across my face, and vigorously nodded my head in agreement while dreaming of punching the werewolf hard in the nose.

"Oh, she did, did she?" Emma's eyes narrowed, clearly not buying his flimsy excuse. She turned her scrutiny on me. "Bull. Astra, you're investigating Albert's death, aren't you? I can see it in your eyes."

"Of course not!" I stretched my mouth into a wide, innocent smile and raised my hands into the air with my palms facing outward. "I'm not investigating anything. Lothian asked if I wanted a drink at the hotel bar." I stared unwaveringly. "Why would I say no?"

"Why would you..." Emma trailed off and stared. "You're both lying to me." She stood with her arms crossed, her mouth set in a hard line as her eyes flicked between us. Her eyebrows were furrowed, her face tight with annoyance.

"Of course we're not," Lothian insisted.

Eddie appeared at her side, and Emma raised

her hands, pointing at us. "They claim they're sneaking off to the bar for drinks. Like a social date thing." Her finger bounced back and forth between us. "Them. Do you believe that?"

Eddie opened his mouth. "I—"

"Well, I don't. I don't believe it at all."

Eddie looked between Lothian and me, his expression unreadable. "Of course I do. They wouldn't lie to you, my love. This weekend is about celebrating the two of—"

Emma glared a warning.

Eddie cleared his throat. "— celebrating you, not chasing mysteries." Eddie looked pointedly at me over Emma's head, a silent warning in his eyes. "Why don't you two go enjoy that drink? Emma and I have guests left to talk to and more mingling to do."

Emma grumbled under her breath, clearly unconvinced. "I'm sure they're lying."

I wasn't sure Bridezilla was sure of anything other than the color pink.

Before Emma could launch into another attack, my sisters materialized out of nowhere to surround her, and Ami looped her arm through Emma's, smiling brightly. "Don't spoil this for them, Emma! Astra finally agreed to give Lothian a real chance. We've been trying to get her out for drinks with him for ages."

No, they hadn't.

Althea nodded, glancing between Emma and me meaningfully. "After everything with Jason, she deserves a bit of fun. Just let her enjoy herself tonight."

"Yes, it's so romantic!" Ayla gushed with as chipper a tone as I'd ever heard come from the mouth of Hades' daughter, clasping her hands together. "The maid of honor and best man getting together on your wedding weekend. Like fate!"

I was never going to live this night down.

Not ever.

Emma's suspicious expression softened, her gaze darting between my siblings. "Well, I suppose you're right. Astra has been really stubborn about not dating. Heck, even Jason's dating in the underworld." Her eyes met mine, a hint of hope flickering in their depths. "And Ayla's right. It would be kind of perfect if you two hit it off this weekend, wouldn't it?"

I stared at Emma in mute horror, my stomach twisting itself into knots and wondering briefly if more of that quiche was left.

Lothian's ego was big enough without all this

encouragement, and with every reinforcing statement, the sexy werewolf practically gloated with smugness. I could feel his eyes on me, and I knew that he was enjoying every bit of this.

There was no gracious way to correct all this misinformation and maintain the cover story that protected Emma from the truth.

That meant I would have to maintain the cover for the whole weekend.

And that stupid werewolf knew it.

I forced a stiff smile, hoping it looked natural. "We'll just see how it goes. It's just drinks. No need to rush into anything."

Emma gave an enthusiastic nod before allowing my sisters to lead her away, chattering excitedly about weddings and romance.

Once she was out of earshot, Eddie looked sternly at us. "Wrap it up as quickly as you can. I can only distract Emma from a case for so long. She already senses something is happening, and if she catches you sneaking and investigating..." He left the warning unspoken, brows lifted in emphasis.

Lothian nodded. "Understood."

I waited until Eddie disappeared into the crowd, too, then glared at Lothian. "I finally agreed to drinks with you? Really? You couldn't think of anything else?"

Lothian smirked, clearly far too amused by the turn of events. "I absolutely could have thought of something else. Come on, Astra. I rather like the idea of fate bringing us together. Drinks, romance..." He waggled his eyebrows playfully. "I wonder if Albert has a king bed in his hotel room."

I balled up my fist and punched Lothian in the arm. "In your dreams. Now let's get to Albert's room before anyone else decides to play matchmaker."

The werewolf chuckled, gesturing for me to lead the way.

# CHAPTER FIVE

*L*othian and I slipped out of the reception hall and hurried across the parking lot toward his flashy black sports car. Within minutes, we were speeding down the road toward the hotel where Uncle Albert (and the other guests) were staying during the wedding weekend.

As Lothian drove, I wondered if I should get a room at the hotel for the remainder of the wedding festivities. Since Emma's brother Rex (and any vampire plus one he may be bringing) could only attend events in the evening, the daytime hours might provide opportunities to speak with guests in a more casual setting.

People's guards tended to lower when away from formality…

…and around booze at the hotel pool.

Lothian's knuckles were white as he gripped the steering wheel and accelerated the car. "Why are you so offended by the idea of going out with me? You wound me, Astra," the werewolf said out of nowhere.

"I wound you? I doubt that." I glanced at him. "I'm not offended by the idea of going out with you. I just don't like you. Why is that so hard for you to comprehend?"

Lothian snorted. "I disagree. I think you do like me. You're just fighting it."

"My no means yes? Is that what you're saying?"

"That's not what I'm saying." He glanced at me. "And I haven't laid a hand on you. I'm just asking a question."

"You're wrong. You're not just asking a question. You're implying I'm playing a game with you with my answers, and I'm not. I don't like men that are cocky and self-assured. Well, wait, that's not really true—I did once. There's a time and a place for men like you, but as a woman coming up on my midthirties, I've been there and done that. I'm tired of it. I don't want games. I could never trust someone who never lets their guard down."

Lothian's knuckles whitened on the steering wheel, his jaw clenching at my blunt assessment. For a few moments, he said nothing. Then he inhaled a deep breath and exhaled slowly. "So you'd rather a man who wears his heart on his sleeve, leaving himself vulnerable and open to manipulation like your recently deceased boyfriend?"

That was a low blow.

Low enough that I figured he was trying to bait me into an argument.

What he expected to accomplish from that?

No idea.

I wasn't sure whether I'd hurt his feelings or he wanted to hurt mine, but I was too tired to get into a back and forth with him. I let my anger at his out-of-line comment go. "I prefer humble, authentic, and balanced."

He snorted.

I shrugged. "You asked. Don't get mad at me for answering honestly."

"I'm not mad at you for anything." Lothian's tone remained even. "Just processing. Not many people are that direct with me."

"Get used to it. Subtlety is not my strong suit."

The corners of Lothian's mouth curved upward. "Now that I believe."

We pulled up to the Embrace Resort, a sprawling garden hotel complex with a stunningly grand pool in the center of four long guest buildings that sparkled like a blue gemstone in a setting of lush tropical foliage that rustled gently in the warm Florida breeze. Meandering walkways wove through the greenery like lazy river tributaries.

Each room boasted a balcony offering an inclusive view of the pool area and the leafy tropical tapestry around it, while every front door spilled out into breezy, open-air corridors overlooking the surrounding parking lot.

Lothian parked his car in an empty space near the end of a row, away from other vehicles. "Not taking any chances of being spotted, I see," I commented.

The Embrace Resort had a relaxed, retro vibe with its stucco arches, red barrel tile roof, and lattice wood accents. In the daylight, it likely appeared vibrant, lush, and inviting. At night, beneath the amber glow of exterior lighting, it seemed a bit worn and mysterious.

"I'd rather avoid complications," Lothian said, shutting off the engine. "Occasionally, the pack would use this place when we needed to lay low. That was before we moved here for Emma, of course. Even though the staff is accustomed to discretion, let's not take any chances."

We exited the car, and Lothian led the way along one of the garden paths toward Albert's room with a confidence that demonstrated his familiarity with the place. I followed close behind, dodging fronds and foliage in the dim lighting until we emerged at the far end of the eastern building.

Lothian swiped the key card in the lock, the mechanism clicking open with a soft beep. He held the door open, gesturing for me to step inside.

"How did you know which room it was?" I asked. "Was it on the card?"

"Eddie let me know. They booked the rooms for everyone."

The musty room was dark, the faint glow of a neon "open" sign on the mini bar providing the only illumination. An uneasy feeling stirred in my gut as I stepped across the threshold and flipped on the light.

The room was nondescript, furnished in browns and tans meant to imply rustic charm. A king-sized bed with a wooden headboard dominated the space, flanked by nightstands. An armchair and small round table occupied one corner near the balcony, while a dresser and desk lined the opposite wall.

The sliding glass door to the balcony stood open, gauzy curtains fluttering in the breeze as if Uncle Albert's spirit still lingered.

I moved slowly through the room, taking in every detail. The decorative touches were sparse. No personal items or knickknacks to provide clues about the occupant. The wastebasket was empty, the surfaces clear of debris. No toothbrush or deodorant on the bathroom sink. No clothes hanging up.

Either Albert traveled very lightly, or someone had performed an extremely efficient cleanup. The room felt empty.

"The room's been wiped down, I think," I told Lothian—which was silly, honestly. The werewolf's sense of smell dwarfed mine. "The question is whether it was just the housekeeping staff preparing the room or someone more recent during this evening." I pointed toward the open glass door. "That makes me think it's a fifty-fifty chance someone visited the room before we did."

Lothian nodded, bending to examine the sink in the bathroom. "Not a single watermark. It's spotless." He straightened, scanning the room with a frown. "Too spotless."

"Not necessarily, though. It depends on when he arrived and how long he spent in here. We need to find out when he checked in." I strode into the bathroom after the werewolf, noting the perfectly folded towels, sparkling mirror, and clean floors. The wastepaper hamper contained not a single tissue or toiletry wrapper.

The tingling in my fingertips intensified the longer we searched the barren room. There might be a story here, a story someone tried to thoroughly and deliberately erase.

Or it was just a newly assigned hotel room.

Luckily, most story's energies lingered, waiting to be rediscovered.

* * *

I MOVED TO THE NIGHTSTAND, laid my bare hand flat against the surface, and closed my eyes. Past the aggressive disinfecting, traces of energy and memory remained. A pen scratching on paper. The snap of a lid on a pill bottle. A stifled cough and ragged breathing. Was it Albert? It was hard to tell, energy layer upon energy layer from so many people. Hotel rooms were like energy convergence epicenters.

I saw his face in the mirror near the bed.

Uncle Albert.

My eyes flew open. "Albert was ill when he checked in. It sounded like he was ill but it could have been a longer-term illness. He was a smoker, after all." I tapped my chest. "It was a chest rattling, mucus or phlegm thing. I heard and felt him rattle when he breathed."

Lothian crossed his arms, brow furrowed. "If that's true, Albert's death tonight may not have been murder. Maybe we're just being paranoid."

"I'm never paranoid."

Lothian held up his hands in mock surrender. "My apologies. I should know better than to question your intuition by now."

"Oh, shut up." I looked around the pristine room again, realizing something was missing. "Do you see Albert's suitcase anywhere? Or anything that looks like personal belongings?"

Lothian frowned, scanning the space. He opened a drawer and closed it once again. "There's nothing here that indicates Albert even stayed in this room. Well, other than your vision."

"Exactly." I approached the open balcony door, peering at the shadowy grounds below.

"And this door was open when we came in. Okay, wolf, do you smell anything off about this room? Anything that doesn't match a normal hotel room?"

I stepped out onto the balcony, hoping to remove my scent a bit.

The werewolf moved silently around the room, pausing by the bed, then near the entrance to the bathroom. His nostrils flared as he breathed long, sorting through the mingled scents. "There's a faint medicinal smell here by the bed. Cough syrup, maybe?"

"That's not adding to what I already saw."

"You didn't ask if I smelled anything different from what you saw." Lothian moved to join me on the balcony, resting his hands on the railing as he stared at the shadowed grounds. The pool was illuminated by soft, white spotlights, giving the water a mysterious and ethereal glow. "So someone took the risk to climb through this balcony, take Albert's suitcase, and leave again?"

"Not much of a risk," I pointed out. "Almost everyone staying at this hotel was at the rehearsal dinner." I frowned, gripping the balcony railing. "Are there any security cameras we can check? Maybe they caught someone entering or leaving with Albert's stuff."

Lothian shook his head. "No cameras. I told you—this hotel cultivates discretion. Many of the usual guests prefer anonymity, if you know what I mean." He glanced pointedly at the rows of rooms and balconies surrounding us. "Werewolves, for one. We value privacy."

Of course.

No self-respecting lycanthrope would want their activities documented.

Lothian paused, gazing at me beneath the silvery glow of moonlight. His blue eyes reflected the shimmering light, and for a moment, his handsome face held an almost predatory cast. "What about your goddess gifts? Can those turn up any clues we might miss?"

As if Lothian's words called to it, I slowly lifted my hands, marveling at how they tingled. A million microscopic fireflies seemed to dance on my fingertips, creating tiny star power bolts that flashed in the darkness. "My goddess gift, as you call it, isn't something specific. I unleash it, and it kind of does what it wants."

"Right, but—"

"I cannot directly control or steer it. It brings justice down on a situation, but ever since Jason died, I've been thinking—whose idea of justice?

Athena's? Astraea's?" I shrugged. "My father Apollo's? What if I disagree?"

Archie's wings flapped silently as he descended from the night sky and gracefully landed on the balcony railing.

"Good evening," I said.

His sharp eyes glinted in the moonlight, and his talons clicked against the railing as he snapped his beak at me in annoyance. "Honestly, I leave you alone for five minutes, and you start spilling your doubts about your powers to any Tom, Dick, or hairy beast that asks. Do I have to watch you constantly?"

I reached out to stroke Archie's head in an attempt to soothe his ruffled feathers—literally. "Calm down, Arch. Lothian already knows a bit about the star power. He knows I'm Apollo's daughter. He knows about Athena. He won't share anything we discuss in confidence. Will you, wolf?"

"I thought you couldn't trust anyone that didn't let their guard down?" Lothian asked. "Have I suddenly been elevated to trustworthy?"

"I think I like you better when you're a wolf and can't talk." Archie's large eyes narrowed with suspicion as he swiveled his head to pin the werewolf with a stern gaze. "You really just don't know when to turn it off, do you, Pennington?"

Lothian lifted his hands, eyebrows furrowed, and lips pursed. He was confident in most situations, but even he knew that getting on the bad side of a nimble owl was not wise. "You're right. Look, I would never betray Astra's trust or reveal sensitive secrets. Just as I would never expect the two of you to do so where pack business is concerned."

Archie ruffled his feathers again and made a disgruntled hooting sound as he fixed me with a look once more. "You need to remember this overgrown pup isn't entitled to goddess knowledge just because he bats his eyes at you. Capiche?" The owl shook himself, pushed off the railing, and fled into the night.

I knew Archie was annoyed he didn't get invited to the wedding, but I don't think I realized how annoyed he was until a minute ago. "Don't take Archie's attitude personally. He wanted to go to the wedding. He also grew up around Greek deities, and they were always fighting and suspicious of each other. Loyalties were constantly changing, and betrayals were around every corner. Archie has difficulty moving past that mindset when in a bad mood."

"Astra, I meant what I said—your secrets are safe with me." Lothian looked down at me with his deep sapphire blue eyes, the hint of pain in their depths unmistakable. "I hope you know that."

Did I know that?

I studied Lothian for a long moment, unsure how to respond.

His loyalty to Emma inspired trust, but the werewolf's motives felt less... straightforward when it came to me. I sensed hidden depths and mysteries beneath his charm, leaving me hesitant about confiding in him completely.

"I appreciate you promising to keep things in confidence, Lothian. But Archie isn't wrong to be cautious. My gifts aren't common knowledge outside our group, and they have weaknesses I'd rather not advertise." Like I didn't know what they would do each time I snapped, crackled, and popped my little lightning bolt fingers. "The goddess hasn't asked me to save someone's life for quite a while, and until she does, let's just pretend I don't have those powers. All right?"

Lothian's jaw tightened, but he gave a slow nod. "I understand. And I don't expect you to share more than you're comfortable with." He leaned against the balcony railing, gazing up at the starry sky, his mouth curved into a wry smile. "And if you want to do it naked, that's fine by me."

\* \* \*

I WALKED BACK INSIDE, annoyed at Lothian's crude joke.

Why did he have to be like that—tactless, inappropriate, his flirting bordering on offensive? The werewolf had charm and charisma to spare, but his sense of humor clearly needed refinement.

His joke about being naked, uttered with a mischievous grin, had knocked me slightly off balance, and I stumbled forward as my foot snagged on a chair leg. I managed to catch the back of the chair just before I fell.

The moment my fingers made contact, a vision overwhelmed my senses.

Albert sat on the bed, his gaze heavy and hesitant as he looked up at Beatrice. She crossed her arms firmly against her chest and set her jaw with determination. A chasm of unspoken words hung in the air between them.

Which was unfortunate, since I couldn't hear unspoken words.

"I already told you, Beatrice, you'll have no

part in the radio station." Albert's body was tense as he stared up at his niece with a determined look in his eye. "It's going to Vincent when I'm gone. I've made my decision. It has to be that way."

Beatrice's eyes lit up with intensity, her cold gaze turning into a bright spark. "None of this makes any sense! Why the sudden change?"

"Vincent has worked for me for over a decade. He's earned the right to take over and will do a fine job of it. You have no experience. All you want is money and status you haven't lifted a finger to achieve! Stop bothering me about it!"

Beatrice leaned forward, jabbing a finger at Albert. "I'm your niece! My father's business should come to me, not get handed over to some conspiracy-spewing DJ you hardly know outside of work."

"You don't know what you're talking about."

If Beatrice actually loved Vincent De Luca, she had a funny way of showing it.

The argument continued, anger and resentment swirling in the air. But the vision changed abruptly as Lothian grabbed my arm and shook me.

"Astra!" His worried gaze searched my face.

"What's wrong? You completely zoned out for a minute. Are you all right?"

I blinked, the present sliding back into focus as the vision released its hold. My fingers still tingled from contact with the chair. "I'm fine. I just..." I moistened my lips, trying to find the right words. "I saw Beatrice and Albert in this room. They were arguing over the radio station. He planned to leave it to Vincent, not Beatrice. She was furious."

Lothian's eyes narrowed. "If Beatrice knew Vincent stood to inherit that radio station, she wouldn't have any motive to see Albert dead."

"But De Luca would."

# CHAPTER SIX

*L*othian and I left Albert's empty hotel room and returned to his sports car. As we slid into the seats, an uneasy silence fell between us. My mind spun with unanswered questions and theories about the strange clues we had uncovered.

"Go to the bar and wait for folks to come in?" I asked.

"Sounds good." Lothian started the engine but then turned it off, turning to look at me with a frown. "Why do you think the room was emptied out? And Albert's belongings taken? Someone must have taken them, right?"

"It could have just been a thief. Maybe he flashed his money around and made himself a target, and it's just a coincidence. Or to hide evidence." I stared out the windshield at the shadowed hotel facade. "Maybe whoever did this wanted to make it appear Albert never checked in. Create confusion? I don't know."

"The staff would have records of his stay, though. They'd know the room was booked in his name. They'd know he checked in."

"True." I drummed my fingers on the armrest, thinking. "What if whoever took his things wanted them for a specific reason? Information or valuables Albert had with him?"

"That's possible." Lothian started the car again and backed out of the parking space, glancing in his mirrors. "Though it seems risky to sneak into a hotel and steal a guest's luggage, even late at night. Seems sloppy."

I nodded, still troubled by the cryptic clues. "Why would Beatrice bring Vincent as her date to the wedding if she was so furious about the possibility of him inheriting Albert's radio station?"

Lothian shot me a sideways look, one eyebrow arched. "Beatrice didn't bring Vincent. He came as Connie's plus one."

"No, that can't be right." I was about to argue but paused and replayed Connie's words. There was no denying it; Lothian was right. "You're right, my mistake. Okay, so wait a minute—Vincent worked for Albert, was inheriting the radio station from him even though cousin Beatrice wanted it, and cousin Connie is dating him, but cousin Beatrice loves him?" I went over it in my head one more time. "Does that sound right? Because to me, it sounds like a spaghetti mess."

Lothian shrugged, glancing at me with an apologetic look. "I'm afraid I'm not entirely clear on the family dynamics or relationships here. Emma doesn't talk about her extended family much, and I wasn't part of the group that worked on seating or invitations."

"Who was?"

"Rex and Norden."

I pulled out my phone, put it on speaker, and called Rex. Emma's vampire brother would know the details we needed, and I'd rather go directly to a family member than another werewolf trying to keep all these Sullivans straight.

After a few rings, Rex answered. "Astra? Is everything all right?"

"Everything's fine, Rex. I just had a couple of questions about your family. Have a minute?"

"Of course, ask away."

"Who are Beatrice's parents?"

"Beatrice Sullivan is the daughter of Blake and Theresa Sullivan," Rex replied. "Blake was my father's brother. Unfortunately, they died in a boating accident while on vacation in Key West when Beatrice was 23."

"Gotcha." That didn't entirely explain why Beatrice felt the radio station should have been left to her, but with her parents gone, maybe Albert was her closest family member. "And who is Connie?"

"Connie Smith is our cousin on our mother's side of the family," Rex said. "Our first cousin. Though she looks younger, Connie is in her late thirties. Her mother, Mildred, is our aunt."

Lothian glanced at me. "So Connie isn't Beatrice's sister, then?"

"No, they're not related by blood," Rex confirmed. "Just through marriage and family connections. However, Aunt Sybil and our mother are quite close, so we saw Connie quite a bit growing up. You likely won't see much of either during the wedding since they're looking after the baby."

The tangled web of relationships was coming into focus.

"One more question," I said. "How long have

Connie and Vincent been seeing each other? Do you know?"

"I have no idea. We saw Connie as children, but this is the first time I've seen her in years. We stopped seeing Connie much after she graduated." I could hear a faint smile in Rex's voice. "I can tell you Aunt Sybil seems quite taken with Vincent, but she's reserving judgment for now. He is rather eccentric, to say the least."

"That's an understatement," I muttered. We'd heard from one of the werewolves that Vincent's enthusiastic theories about paranormal conspiracies and government cover-ups had dominated his assigned table's dinner conversation. "If I told you that I think Beatrice was also seeing Vincent, what would you say to that?"

A pause. "I've watched all of them all evening, and I can overhear far more than your average person attending the wedding," Rex replied, mildly confused. "Nothing in Beatrice and Vincent's interaction with one another would lead me to believe they were romantically involved."

Lothian and I exchanged a look. "Could your vision be wrong?" he asked me.

I glared at him.

"Sorry. It was just a question. Maybe it meant something else."

Rex's information seemed to point to Beatrice, Vincent, and possibly Connie as suspects in Uncle Albert's early demise, but other than unexplained connections and hypothetical greed motivations, the clues were sparse.

I sighed, dragging a hand through my hair. "Thanks for clarifying, Rex. Family connections can be hard to follow."

"You don't have to tell me twice." Rex chuckled. "Let me know if you have any other questions. And do try to enjoy what's left of the evening! This is supposed to be a celebration."

The call ended, and I slipped my phone into my pocket with a frown.

We were left with several shaky motives but few certain clues pointing to the culprit behind Uncle Albert's demise—if it was murder.

Which we still didn't know.

Well, I knew.

No one chokes on a fluffy quiche.

* * *

LOTHIAN and I entered the hotel's tiki lounge, The Palm Frond, just off the main reception area. The walls, accented with pink and emerald green silk palm fronds, were painted blindingly bright turquoise that glowed obnoxiously under black accent lights. Natural moonlight filtered through the glass ceiling illuminating the room with a cool hue. The vivid pink chairs between potted tropical plants at small tables added a Barbie Jungle-like atmosphere.

The place was hideous, and I felt like I would have nightmares about pink until my old age.

Lothian led me to a small table and waved to the bartender. He pointed two fingers at us with a charming smile, motioning for a drink.

"What can I get for you both?"

Without waiting for my input, the werewolf ordered some tropical-sounding umbrella cocktail for me and a whiskey straight up for himself. I shot him a glare before canceling the fruity frozen concoction (that would likely be pink), asking the bartender for a vodka cranberry instead.

The bartender nodded and quickly bustled away.

Lothian arched a brow. "Are you being contrary just to be contrary?"

"I'm ordering for myself because I'm an independent person," I replied, meeting his gaze evenly. "I don't need a man deciding what I want."

Lothian's eyes narrowed as he cocked his head to the side, studying me like a scientist observing a new species. A grimace twisted his lips, but it couldn't hide the mischievous twinkle in his eyes. "I'm going to ask you a question, and I hope you don't storm out of here in a huff—but I'm so curious, I'm willing to risk it." He leaned back in his chair. "Do you really think someone did Uncle Albert in tonight, or are you just occupying yourself for the weekend so you don't have to think about weddings, romance, and all that?"

I gritted my teeth and clenched my fists as I pinned him with a glare. His words stung my pride, and it took all the strength I had not to explode in rage at his insult. "Are you serious?"

"I generally am." We locked eyes in silence. "Well, sometimes."

My face flushed, fists clenched, and my jaw tightened as I glared at him. "Do you go out of your way to be offensive? Because, honestly, I think Archie is right. It really feels like you work at it."

"Sometimes, yes. But not at the moment." Lothian tapped the table lightly with his index finger before leaning forward, his face softening as he met my eyes. "I didn't mean to offend. You sometimes forget that I was in the underworld with you and your sisters. I know what you've been through recently. What I asked was a serious question, not an attack."

"Could have fooled me."

He nodded slightly as if to show he was listening. "I just wondered if wishful thinking might be coloring your views, that's all. I thought maybe..." His expression shifted from concentration to contemplation before finally settling in resignation as he shrugged his shoulders and sighed. "Never mind. I can see I'm just making you angry."

My drink arrived, and I took a long swallow, letting the cool cranberry and alcohol temper the flare of annoyance his words had ignited. I didn't want to admit it, but I knew that Lothian angered me because he wasn't entirely wrong in his assessment.

As much as I was happy for Emma and Eddie, the sea of pink wedding decorations, the ornamental flower arrangements everywhere I turned, and that ubiquitous syrupy rose-hued romantic aura that was choking me like some cloying perfume was making me feel more than a bit nauseated. And yes, every once in a while, I felt practically suffocated by the sea of pastel tulle and gardenia-scented candles for no particular reason I could name.

But Lothian was mistaken if he believed I would see murder in a fat man's quiche bite simply as a diversion or out of resentment.

I set my glass on the table, composing my response. "You're not wrong that I'm finding Emma's wedding a little challenging to navigate. But I would never manufacture a murder case to avoid my discomfort."

"I apologize, then."

"The visions implied foul play," I continued.

"I understand."

I could feel my face, a tense mask of purpose and... something else. Something in me that wanted him to understand what I was saying. I wanted him to believe me. Why did I care if he believed me?

I didn't know.

But for some reason, I did.

"Whatever I'm feeling, though, this isn't about Jason or my considerable issues with romance. It's about catching a murderer—if there is one to be caught—and unearthing the truth about his murder. Whatever that truth may be."

"I understand. And again, you have my

apologies." Lothian's blue eyes shone in the light, twinkling like stars. His face was soft, and his lips curved into a slight smile as he gazed into my eyes. "I didn't mean to insult you with what I said. I'm just concerned that you feel such guilt for what Jason went through that—"

My unyielding glare silenced him as if he sensed from my expression that he was about to tread a step too far—but his words had already struck a nerve.

The words 'Jason' and 'guilt' in the same sentence would probably always drive a knife through my heart. Love came with loss, I reminded myself, and Jason wasn't letting his loss stop him in the underworld.

Of course, he was only there because of me.

I took another sip of my drink, unsure how to navigate this turn in the conversation. My past, the underworld, Jason's death, what my mother had done and kept secret… All these things were complex enough to work through without adding tangled emotions and attraction to a werewolf into the mix.

Yet there sat Lothian watching me with those soulful blue eyes, practically daring me to let my guard down… while holding his guard firmly in place.

* * *

THE BAR DOOR creaked open before either of us could speak, and a tall figure stepped inside. Lothian's eyes widened, then he turned and watched the stranger scan the bar with calm authority.

I frowned. "What's wrong? What—or who —is it?"

Lothian's nostrils flared as he drew in a long breath. "Cough syrup. I smell the same medicinal scent from Albert's hotel room."

My eyes darted to the tall, middle-aged man that had just entered the lounge. His shoulders were tense as he looked around the room, and his gait was purposeful as he made a beeline for an unoccupied table in the far corner stopping just long enough to throw a coffee cup into the garbage.

A few pairs of eyes glanced at him as he passed by before resuming their conversation, but no one displayed any hint of recognition.

He glided into a corner booth with the fluid ease of a seasoned ballet dancer. His back found the security of the wall, and his gaze was trained on the entrance door.

Leaning forward, he adopted a pose I knew all

too well. It was a pose that exuded an air of casual nonchalance, a deceptive veneer concealing a well-honed instinct for defense. A posture so deeply ingrained into my training that it was as reflexive as a knee-jerk reaction. It turned the humble booth into a bird's-eye observation deck.

Lothian waved, gesturing for the bartender. "Is that gentleman with the wedding party? I feel like I've seen him before, but I can't place the name. Don't want to embarrass myself by not remembering a cousin."

The bartender's eyes bored into Lothian with a hard, intense gaze. "I apologize, sir, but you know we do not disclose information about our guests." He wiped the table with a rag, grabbed my empty glass, and then casually walked away without another word.

I arched a brow at Lothian. "You weren't kidding about the discretion here."

"It was worth a try." Lothian sighed, shaking his head. "My mistake, though. I should have known better than to ask him outright." He shot a glance at the stranger. "But that cough syrup scent is too similar to be a coincidence. What are the odds he visited Albert's room or came in contact with the same source?"

"High enough to warrant keeping an eye on

him if you're sure it's the same." The bartender swooped by, leaving another vodka cranberry in front of me.

I took another sip of my drink.

The lingering cough syrup odor pointed to some connection between this stranger and Albert's final hours. But what sort? An accomplice cleaning up evidence? A concerned friend coming to check on Albert before he passed? Without more context, the clue only added another question mark.

Lothian's gaze remained fixed on the stranger. "Think you can get a reading off him without making direct contact?"

I glanced at the garbage can.

"No, but yes. Give me a minute."

I gracefully slid off my chair, making sure not to make too much noise. I moved quickly toward the large metal garbage can near the entrance where I had seen the man hurl his empty paper coffee cup. Taking a quick peek around to make sure no one was watching, I grabbed it from the trash and hurried back to the table.

"Gross," I muttered as I returned to Lothian.

"Worth it if it works."

I held the cup below the small table in my lap. I could feel the energy in the cup, a collective and interwoven set of memories from all those involved in its making. I shut my eyes and sifted through the various threads from paper makers and bean roasters, searching for any recent remnants connected to the man.

A hazy image flickered to life—the stranger sitting across from Albert on the edge of a bed, worry etched into his features. He held out an open pill bottle, tapping two caplets into Albert's wrinkled palm.

"You need to go to the doctor, Albert. Those coughing fits are getting worse."

Albert snorted, swallowing the pills with a grimace. "And they'll say what? That I smoke and I drink, and I eat too much? They'll just tell me to eat right and quit smoking. They'll follow it up with a demand to exercise. None of which I'm gonna do. I've got what I need."

"You'd get a proper diagnosis and treatment." The stranger shoved the pill bottle back into his bag, frustration evident in every line of his body. "Your stubbornness is going to be the death of you, old man. Call me if you change your mind...or if things get worse."

The vision faded, and I blinked as the present swam back into focus. My hands still tingled with energy as I turned to Lothian.

"I saw him with Albert before he passed. He was worried about Albert's deteriorating health and trying to convince him to go to a doctor." I nodded toward the stranger. "Maybe he's just a concerned friend or associate. I didn't smell cough syrup, but my nose isn't as sensitive as yours."

Lothian's brow furrowed. "Do you think he went there after Albert died?" Without waiting for me to answer, Lothian kept on. "No, you would have said something." He dragged a hand through his hair, exhaling in frustration. "None of this makes sense."

I nodded, stymied by the meaningless paths and tangles of clues.

# CHAPTER SEVEN

The bar was suddenly abuzz with newly returning guests arriving back from Emma and Eddie's rehearsal dinner. Groups of family and friends in their formal attire flooded the room, talking animatedly about the wedding and reminiscing about the evening's dramatic (and very pink) events.

Lothian glanced around. "The rehearsal dinner must be over." He tilted his head, brow furrowing. "Come to think of it, I don't remember rehearsing anything. What did we rehearse?"

I smiled, shaking my head at his expression. "A rehearsal dinner isn't really about rehearsing. I mean, it is, but it's really a pre-wedding dinner, usually the night before the ceremony, where the wedding party, close family, and friends come together to toast the bride and groom. The name is a bit misleading."

"Ah, I see." Lothian nodded, understanding dawning. "A tradition I was unaware of." He flashed a roguish grin. "Our courtships are rather less complex."

"I don't doubt that." I took another sip of my drink, watching as Emma's friends and family filled the lounge, laughter, and good cheer dispersing the somber mood from earlier. A pang of guilt struck me that I couldn't seem to muster the same lighthearted enthusiasm for the sparkly celebrations.

I mean, these people had a family member croak in front of them, and they were in a better mood than I was.

I put down my glass and frowned.

Was Lothian correct?

Did I search out mystery and purpose to avoid facing the grief and discomfort this wedding weekend had stirred in me?

I swirled the remains of my drink, troubled by the possibility—and the possibility Lothian had pegged me before I'd recognized my own motivations.

I didn't think so. Ami had mentioned she'd felt something off at the dinner, too. It wasn't just my instinct sending up alarm bells, I told myself as I took a long sip of the tart drink, feeling the burn in my throat. No star card was glowing in Ami's hand this weekend, no Athena-powered flashing demand with some deified celestial power pushing me in directions I didn't want to go. This was just me sensing something was off about Uncle Albert's death.

It had nothing to do with my feelings about Emma's wedding.

Right?

Wyatt Marlow strode into the smoky bar with a purpose, his broad shoulders and tall frame standing out in the crowd. He held tightly to my sister Ami's hand as they made their way through the throng of people toward our small table. "I thought I'd find you both here," Wyatt said.

"And so you have." Lothian gestured to a nearby booth. "Join us?"

We shuffled over to the booth, its pink vinyl-covered seats glowing in the black light. Ami slid in after me and bumped my shoulder before tucking a lock of light blond hair behind her ear. "Althea and Ayla went home. They were annoyed they couldn't get into the bar yet."

"I wonder who's more annoyed about what they can't do tonight, our sisters or Archie?"

"Archie," Ami said. "I think I saw him sulking in a tree out front."

Wyatt leaned in toward Lothian. "Emma and Eddie returned to the house. Norden and Lawrence are standing guard."

"Standing guard?" I raised an eyebrow. "It's a wedding, not an invasion."

"Well, it's kind of both," Ami said, gesturing at the crowded bar.

"At least Emma's in a defensible castle, even if it's part werewolf frat house."

Lothian's gaze was fixed sternly on Wyatt, and he acted as if he hadn't even heard my flippant comment about a werewolf frat house. "When you walked in here, what did you make of the man in the corner? I caught a whiff of the same medicinal scent from Albert's hotel room on him, and he seems like he's on alert for something."

Swiftly, Wyatt's gaze shifted to lock onto the unfamiliar face. "I didn't detect anything unusual about him but wasn't paying close attention. He seemed occupied with his drink and phone." Wyatt looked back at Lothian. "Do you suspect him of something?"

"We're not certain." Lothian described the

clues uncovered in Albert's hotel room, the stranger's timely arrival with a noticeable cough syrup scent, and my reading of the man's coffee cup. "It may be a coincidence, but it's an odd one. And after what Astra sensed from Albert's body at the rehearsal dinner..."

Wyatt's eyebrows drew together, forming a deep line on his forehead. "Emma said Albert choked on his food. Are you saying that wasn't an accident?"

"It was a quiche," I said with emphasis on the word 'quiche' and an accompanying hand gesture to indicate that there was no doubt in my mind that this was no accident.

Wyatt stared at me. "I don't understand."

"Quiche is literally listed on a handout from the Muscular Dystrophy Association as a meal to make for easy swallowing if someone is prone to choking. It's listed in bold right along with applesauce and mashed potatoes. I find it hard to believe Albert choked on a piece of quiche," I replied.

"Is that true?" Lothian asked me.

"You have a phone. Look it up." I turned back to Wyatt. "I know everyone thinks it's accidental, but when I touched Albert, it seemed more like he had an allergic reaction than he choked. He took one bite and immediately started coughing —and that wasn't the first piece of quiche he had. I think someone spiked that mini-quiche with something he was allergic to."

"She's right," Lothian said, holding up his phone. "Well, I don't know about the spiking part, but quiche is recommended for people with medical conditions that make swallowing difficult."

"You think the police will check into it?" Ami asked.

I shook my head. "I doubt most of the men on the police force know what a quiche is, much less how choke-able a piece of it would be."

Wyatt leaned back in the booth, exhaling a long breath. "What you say makes sense, but what you say is also made up almost entirely of supposition, circumstantial evidence, and psychic observation. Without clear evidence, we can't make unfounded accusations in the middle of Emma's wedding weekend."

I loved how even Eddie's best men and groomsmen considered the bubblegum-colored weekend Emma's wedding first, Eddie's wedding second.

"Not that we have anyone to accuse." Wyatt glanced at Lothian. "We'll need to keep an eye on this stranger, though, and dig quietly into his identity and background."

"Agreed," Lothian said to his packmate.

Ami raised her eyebrow. "If that guy is staying here at the hotel, one of us should probably get a room for the weekend to keep an eye out." She glanced at Wyatt. "We can do it."

"The place is completely booked for the weekend," I told her. "There's not one room available, much less two rooms."

"Well, there is one room available. Wyatt and I can stay in Uncle Albert's room. You said you had the key, Lothian, and the room's already reserved for the wedding weekend, right?" She gave me a hopeful look. "I can do some readings while there."

Wyatt fixed his gaze on the tabletop, staring intently at the intricate wood grain. His cheeks were flushed, and he shifted in his chair, unable to meet anyone's eyes.

"Lothian and I will stay in Albert's room for the weekend," I said instinctively and entirely without thinking.

* * *

I SENSED the attraction between Ami and Wyatt (who was way too old for my sister) and reacted in the moment without thinking—and without thinking through the implications of Lothian and I staying in a hotel room together for an entire wedding weekend.

With one king-sized bed.

I'd realized my mistake pretty quickly, but there was nothing I could do.

There was no easy way to get out of it.

Lothian expertly navigated his car through the hotel complex, eventually stopping in front of the ivy-covered building we'd previously visited. We stepped out into the warm evening air, and he opened the trunk with the press of a button.

"I just realized you don't have anything with you," Lothian said. "Should we run to your house?"

"I'll be fine."

He grabbed a duffel bag from the back, its leather straps creaking as he slung it over his shoulder. The headlights of the cars in the parking lot cast a faint yellow glow on Lothian's facial features. His eyes seemed to sparkle.

His overnight bag was surprisingly small, sturdy, and nondescript. Not what I imagined for such a flashy werewolf. "Is that a bug-out bag for emergencies or a regular overnight bag for... uh, less urgent emergencies?"

"You never know when an emergency might arise," he said, his voice low and husky. "But this," he added, gesturing to the bag, "is just a regular overnight bag. Or are you asking if I had it handy because I need it often?"

"I didn't—"

"You didn't, but there was an implication there."

I snorted. "Don't flatter yourself."

His grin widened as he slammed the trunk closed and slung the bag over his shoulder. "A werewolf learns to be prepared for any eventuality. We ruin a lot of clothes when we shift. But as to your implication, no—I don't habitually spend the night with every woman I spend time with. If that's what you were implying." His eyes glinted with amusement as we made our way to the room.

I quickly looked away, hoping the shadows would hide my red cheeks. Lothian seemed determined to challenge me with every step we took, but I refused to let him see that he was getting under my skin. I ignored his flirtations, keeping my eyes straight ahead in a stoic stare.

Lothian's hand trembled slightly as he slid the

key card into the slot and watched it light up green. The door groaned, creaking open to reveal Uncle Albert's dark room. He stepped aside, motioning for me to go in first.

The space was unchanged from our earlier visit, still barren of personal belongings and smelling strongly of disinfectant. Lothian set his bag on the dresser and strode to the balcony doors, sliding them open to allow fresh air to circulate.

I shifted my weight nervously, my eyes drawn to the large king bed in the center of the room. The armchair I had already chosen was far too soft for my liking, and I knew it would be hard to sleep in. But I was going to anyway: "You should take the bed. I'll stay in the chair. I'm ex-military. I can sleep anywhere."

Lothian spun around to face me. "No, no. That would be silly. We're adults, and the bed is plenty big enough for both of us." He softened his features, a hint of concern etching his face. "Unless that idea makes you uncomfortable?"

I averted my gaze, staring at the patterned carpet.

Was I uncomfortable sharing a bed with Lothian?

His question hung in the air like a cloud of smoke, polluting my already turbulent feelings.

Part of me wanted to get away from him before I got dragged into the vortex of emotions that threatened to break through my carefully constructed and compartmentalized walls. This wasn't a good idea, I told myself, but there seemed no escaping it. My relationship with Emma and her marriage to Eddie was stubbornly insisting on pulling me further and further into Lothian Pennington's orbit.

Yet despite the warning bells going off inside me, I couldn't ignore the spark of electricity that connected us every time we looked at each other or the magnetism that pulled me closer even when my better judgment screamed at me to stay away.

Better to keep a cautious distance, even in close quarters, I thought.

That settled it.

I would sleep in the chair.

After this comprehensive and in-depth conversation with myself (where I decided on the best course of action), I cleared my throat, met his gaze with a shrug of forced indifference, and said, "Sure, let's share. It's a big bed. I'm sure we can maintain appropriate personal space."

Because clearly, I'm an idiot.

Lothian tossed a folded t-shirt and pair of boxer shorts onto the bed. "Here. Since you didn't bring anything to sleep in, I have extra. I try to be prepared for any situation."

I stared at the offering, hesitating.

Wearing Lothian's clothes seemed an intimacy I wasn't certain I was ready for. I touched the t-shirt, and my imagination suddenly conjured images of waking in the middle of the night, the two of us accidentally tangled together... It set my pulse racing in a way I didn't care to examine too closely.

But my options were limited, and I had to admit the fancy rehearsal dinner dress was uncomfortable when I was upright—I doubted sleeping in the thing would be any better.

With a quiet sigh of resignation, I grabbed the t-shirt and shorts. "Thanks. I'll return these washed."

Lothian flashed a quick grin, apparently satisfied I'd accepted his goodwill gesture. "No need. I have more."

His nonchalance was enviable.

I slipped into the small bathroom to change, comforted by the knowledge that the werewolf's keen senses wouldn't detect the riot of confusion this situation had ignited within me. By the time I emerged, he was sprawled across his half of the expansive bed, politely leaving a cavernous space between us.

The hours until sunrise stretched before us, and as I crawled into bed, dawn seemed a long way off.

* * *

I LAY PARALYZED with fear as Jason's face contorted with rage. Fire shot from his eyes as he spoke, spewing his words like venom. "Your meddling cost me my life! If you hadn't been so distant, I'd still be here." His words cut into me like a knife.

Guilt tore through me like a riptide as dream-Jason's angry voice rang in my ears, and he shook his fist at me. Tears streamed down my face, blurred vision making it hard to see him. "It was never meant to be this way! I'm so sorry, Jason!" My voice cracked as I desperately begged for forgiveness.

Jason's features shifted and twisted into those of his mother, her eyes narrowed with rage. She was pointing a gun at me, her mouth contorted into a cruel smirk as she spoke. "It's your fault my son is lying in his grave! Now you'll get what you deserve!"

I watched in horror as she clicked the hammer back, her eyes locked on me. "This isn't right!" I shouted. Tears streamed down my face as I pleaded with her. "Please don't do this! My sisters need me!"

I shot upright in the bed, my heart pounding against my ribcage. The room was cloaked in shadow, illuminated only by streaks of silver light from the moon slipping through the lace curtains. Beside me, Lothian sat up.

"Astra?" His voice was rough but laced with concern. "Are you all right?"

I took a shaky breath, dragging a hand through my sleep-tousled hair. The remnants of the nightmare swirled around me like a fog, threatening to pull me back into its dark depths. "Just a bad dream," I said softly. "Go back to sleep. I'm sorry I woke you."

The only light came from the window, casting Lothian's imposing figure in shadow. His voice was gentle but firm. "I heard you calling for Jason, and then it sounded like you were talking to someone who wanted to hurt you. What's going on?"

"It's fine." I sighed, grasping for composure.

"His mother. In the nightmare, she blamed me for Jason's death. Well, not just in the nightmare. She pulled a gun on me once." I gave a mirthless laugh. "Anyway, I'm fine. Really."

The bed creaked as Lothian inched closer, his muscled body pressing against my side. His eyes searched my face as he tentatively reached out and touched my arm, a feather-light grip that barely held me. "You can't keep blaming yourself for what happened to Jason," he murmured tenderly. "It wasn't your fault."

"Wasn't it?" I held Lothian's gaze, willing him to understand.

"No."

"You're wrong."

"I'm not."

"You are. I got involved with him knowing he was just a human and my world was an absolute magical mess. I kept him at arm's length so I couldn't fully protect him, but I pulled him in close enough that he was at risk from all the garbage swirling around me, thanks to my mother. Garbage I, like an idiot, didn't even see until it was too late. And when I finally realized what she had done to us, he paid the price for being with me before I could react. Before I could save anyone." My voice broke on the final words.

"So, you're wrong. His death is absolutely my fault."

Lothian gently encircled me with his arm, pulling me against his strong chest. His warmth cocooned me as I tried to fight back the tears that stung my eyes.

"You can't control the actions of others or be blamed when their obsessions and poor choices lead to ruin," Lothian said softly. "Your mother made her decisions. Jason made his decisions. They came with consequences neither you nor anyone else could have prevented." He stroked my hair soothingly, and I melted into him, feeling safe for one fleeting moment even as I warred within myself whether to stay in his embrace or retreat. "Emma told me that he's released you from blame, from any anger. If he's let it go, you should, too. He wouldn't want you to live like this."

I let Lothian's words envelop me, dulling the raw pain that had consumed my dreams. His strong arms felt like an anchor in the storm-tossed sea of my emotions, and I leaned into his embrace.

I have no idea how long we sat like that, but I finally exhaled, cheeks flushed with embarrassment, and slowly disengaged from the warm embrace. I lightly patted his chest with a trembling hand as I searched for the right words. "I'm really sorry. I don't normally crumble like that."

With tenderness, Lothian brushed a stray lock of hair from my cheek, causing the warmth in his touch to spread throughout my body. His eyes glimmered with compassion as he spoke in a low, soothing voice. "We all need to fall apart sometimes," he murmured, his thumb lightly grazing my skin. "Especially when we've been through what you have." He leaned in closer and continued, "Get some rest. We can talk more in the morning if you'd like. And if you don't want to talk about it, that's okay, too."

Lothian moved back to his side of the bed without argument, leaving me to settle in alone, but his radiating warmth chased away the gnawing guilt that tried once more to prey upon me, and I finally fell into a dreamless sleep.

# CHAPTER EIGHT

The loud knock on the door made my eyes flutter open, and I groggily propped myself up in bed as Lothian crossed the room bare-chested to answer it. He opened the door to reveal Wyatt and Ami, illuminated by the bright morning Florida sun behind them.

"Good morning! Is my sister still sleeping?" Ami sang as she held up one large duffel bag in one hand and two garment bags in the other. "Brought her a few changes of clothes and her maid of honor dress." She swept into the room, Wyatt behind her, without being invited. "I figured you didn't want to wear the same thing two days in a row."

I blinked away the shards of sleep clinging to

my eyes and sat up, taking a few moments to orient myself in the dimly lit room. "Thanks. How's Archie doing?" I asked.

"He came home and slept on his perch in your room most of the night." Ami carefully placed the duffel bag down and hung up the garment bags on a hook near the desk. She reached out and flipped the switch on the lamp, and the room lit up with a warm yellow glow. "You should have seen him eating his bacon this morning. He was scowling and barely touched it. It's safe to say he's still in a mood."

Wyatt glanced at Ami. "Did you tell her what Althea found out?"

Ami shook her head. "Obviously not. I just walked in. You heard everything I said to her. We don't telepathically send messages to one another, you know. Besides, we just opened the doors and got them out of bed. Let's give them a few moments to wake up and let them get some coffee first."

Yes.

Coffee first.

I stumbled out of bed and dragged myself to the dresser, flipping on the full-size coffee maker while praying it would be enough of a jolt of caffeine to get me started with the day. All I could feel was exhaustion after last night's emotional overload and little-to-no sleep.

I turned around once the steaming brown liquid began slowly filling the carafe. "All set," I said.

"What did Althea uncover about our mystery man from the bar?" Lothian asked.

Ami pulled out a folder and then hopped on the bed. "His name is Simon Kincaid. According to public records, he owns a small holistic health store in Orlando." She looked up. "Althea hacked into the hotel registration system and found that Mr. Kincaid is staying on the third floor for the full wedding weekend. Let's not mention that to Emma."

"He's not any kind of doctor?" I asked.

"Nope."

I frowned. "Albert lives—or lived—in Orlando, didn't he?"

"I think so." Wyatt crossed his arms. "It seems odd that he showed up right after Albert's death —and with the cough syrup smell clinging to his clothes. But could it be a coincidence? I mean, he did sell natural remedies. A menthol smell could be any number of things."

The coffee pot on the counter sputtered and

choked, then quivered and beeped like a tired old machine needing rest.

I got up and poured coffee for everyone, handing the mugs around before sliding back into my seat. "I saw a vision of Simon in this room talking to Albert, worried about his health and trying to convince him to see a doctor. But he handed him a pill, not a spoon full of cough syrup or some herbal thing."

"Some herbal things come in pills," Ami said.

I raised my eyebrow. "And smell like cough syrup?"

"Maybe. Althea could say better than I could."

Lothian's brow furrowed. "Is Simon on the guest list?"

Ami and Wyatt shrugged.

"Good question." I sipped my coffee, mulling over the new pieces of the puzzle. There were still too many gaps and contradictions to declare Simon a definite suspect or rule him out completely based on a single connection. My power insisted on drawing my attention to him, yet—as usual—the clues refused to align neatly.

The vision of Simon felt significant, a starting point on this twisting path rather than an end.

Ami's fingers danced over the screen of her phone like a pianist playing a concerto. "I texted

Althea to see if she could get back into the reservation system. If she can, she'll see if Simon's room is coded to the wedding." Then, she flipped open the folder, eyes skimming the documents within. "He's not married. In fact, he's never been married. I don't see any college. No certifications." She glanced up at me. "And just to confirm, no, nothing in this indicates he's any kind of homeopathic doctor or spiritual healer or anything."

I glanced at my watch, its second hand ticking incrementally forward, and then raised my arm to point to the stack of papers Ami held. "Does it have an address for his shop? We could start there and see if anything looks out of place. We could also swing by Albert's place on the way back and poke around."

"Yeah, I've got the address." Ami slid the paper across the table. "But Althea thought the same."

I raised an eyebrow.

"That visiting the shop might be a good idea, especially since Simon's away for the wedding. She and Ayla were going to check it out this morning since they have Aunt Gwennie's Jeep. You want me to tell them to skip it or add Albert's condo to their itinerary?"

I thought about it for a moment, then shook

my head. "No, tell Althea and Ayla to go ahead to Simon's shop and to stop by Albert's. Lothian and I will probably be able to find more useful information at the pool today."

Wyatt glanced between us. "We can accompany them if you'd like. Althea and Ayla. Just to be safe."

"Okay, sounds good." Lothian stood, but Ami's voice stopped him.

"Astra?" She had a serious look in her eyes, and her slender fingers nervously toyed with the edge of the blanket. "Before we all go our separate directions, do you think we could talk? Just the two of us?"

Lothian looked back and forth between me and Ami before settling back into his seat. "I'll finish my coffee and work out the logistics with Wyatt for the day."

* * *

"LET'S TAKE A BREAK OUT HERE," Ami said as we stepped onto the balcony.

A blast of warm air hit us and brought with it the scents of coconut and chlorine mixed with the sweet bouquet of summer flowers in bloom. The sun was high in the blue sky, illuminating the pool with glittering rays that sparkled on the rippling water below us.

Below, cheerful wedding guests in bathing suits hurried through the lush foliage-lined pathways that snaked through the landscape. Some sat on lounges reading magazines; others tapped their feet to island music playing over hidden speakers.

My sister turned and looked at me, her pale face creased with lines of concern. "Astra, can we talk about last night? I have to ask you something."

I leaned against the railing, crossing my arms. "Sure, what's on your mind?"

"You insisted on staying in the hotel room last night only because I wanted to spend some time alone with Wyatt, didn't you?"

"No, that wasn't why." Well, that wasn't the only reason, I thought. "I wanted to investigate the room, see what images I got from other items. It had nothing to do with you and Wyatt."

"Really?" Ami raised her eyebrow. "And did you?"

"Did I…?"

"Get images off other items you forgot to tell us about?"

Oops.

My body tensed, and my stomach dropped as my sister caught me in the lie. I glanced around, attempting to hide the betrayal written on my face with an unconvincing shrug. "Yeah, uh, I was just really tired last night," I said awkwardly. "I'll work on it after we return from the pool."

"Uh-huh." Then Ami sighed.

"What's that sigh for?"

"Astra, you realize I could've just brought Wyatt home to Arden House, gone back to the werewolf castle, or rented a hotel room in any of the hundreds of hotels in Central Florida if I wanted alone time with him, right? I didn't have to stay in this room for that alone time."

"I know that." Well, I didn't think of it until she said it, but now it seemed pretty obvious. If there was one thing Central Florida had an abundance of, it was hotel rooms. "I didn't offer to stay here for your benefit." I turned to look out at the pool, watching a few early morning swimmers doing laps. "It was about the case."

"The case that's not really a case?" Ami moved closer, lowering her voice. "Look, if you want to pretend you didn't react possessively like you did, that's fine, but I'm the psychic seer sister, Astra. I know you did."

"I didn't—"

"You did. And you did because you feel some responsibility to step into Mom's shoes as the oldest sister. I get it. Remember, I was the oldest sister the whole time you were gone. You were just the sister in the military that never came home to visit and that the rest of us barely knew."

Ouch.

True.

But ouch.

I cringed, my face contorting as if I had just taken a bite out of a lemon. "I thought you were the gentle, sweet sister?" I half-heartedly quipped.

"I'm the sister that can see through your bull, Astra, and I'm not the only one." Ami's expression grew serious. "Just promise me one thing. Don't slip into being controlling or meddling with us and thinking that's love. That was Mom's mistake. I'm an adult, and so is Althea, even if she's still learning. Ayla's always been older than her years—on top of having Aunt Gertie and every other ghost in Florida up her butt all the time. You need to respect our choices and our privacy. We're not going to put up with someone not respecting us again. You taught us we don't have to."

My insides tightened, and a surge of guilt washed over me, but it was almost nothing when attached to the chains of remorse I already wore like a noose.

Ami was right, though. She wasn't a naive teen anymore; she was an adult woman making choices.

Who was I to stop her?

But I had stopped her, my conscience whispered.

I could deny all I wanted, but Ami and I knew it was a lie, and she was right. My sisters needed to spread their wings, not be smothered under mine like I was my mother's replacement.

I inhaled and let the air out slowly.

"I'm trying to do better." My voice came out calmer than expected. "You're all growing up, and you didn't have a chance to live on your own terms when Mom was around. I know that. It's ironic—before she passed away, I would have been the first person arguing for you to live on your own terms, by your own choices."

"Yep. I love you, Astra, but sometimes you're so dense." She paused, her expression growing soft. "I was really messed up after Mom died. So messed up. I wasn't sure I would come out of it. You helped me through it—but you can't replace helping everyone else for helping yourself. It's obvious to everyone but you how much Jason's death really shook you and how you haven't begun to deal with what Mom did."

I started to protest, but she shook her head. "No. Don't talk. Just listen. You don't always have to be the strong one, Astra. The weight of the world isn't on your shoulders alone. You have family and friends to help. And you have Archie. You even have your father. You can lean on us when things get hard."

All I could do was offer her a weak smile and an even weaker response: "I know."

Another lie.

"Just don't forget we're here." Ami gave my hand a quick squeeze.

"I won't." My jaw clenched, and I straightened my back, trying to use the tension in my shoulders to steel myself against my inner turmoil.

Ami's piercing gaze seemed to see through the facade covering my doubt and heartache hidden below the surface. "I don't believe you, but we'll see how it goes." She leaned against the railing next to me. "Speaking of how things went, how did it go with you and the werewolf last night?"

"What do you mean?"

"What do you mean 'what do I mean?' I see how Lothian looks at you and how you look at him. I think the air heats up five degrees when you stand beside each other."

A flush crept up my neck at her words. "You're imagining things."

"If you say so. But I want you to know that you don't have to avoid him or pretend there's nothing between you. We're all supportive of you moving on—"

"Lothian and I are just friends. And barely that," I repeated. My voice was stern, and I hoped it conveyed a finality I didn't feel.

Ami held up her hands in defeat. "Okay, okay. I'll drop it."

"Good."

"For now. But I'm here if you ever want to talk about it." Ami linked her arm through mine as we headed for the sliding glass door. "May the grapevine today be fruitful."

"So it shall be." I offered her a small smile.

I knew she meant well, but I wasn't ready to examine my feelings for Lothian.

Or deal with the storm of residual emotions from Jason's death.

Or deal with my father, the god Apollo, in any capacity.

And the less I thought of my mother, the better.

Not yet.

Not now.

Right now, I needed to focus on solving Albert's murder.

The rest?

It could wait.

* * *

Lothian and I descended the wide staircase to the pool area, a man-made rainforest oasis. We were greeted by the thick humidity of the air and a cacophony of sounds: laughter, splashing, and Caribbean-style music playing over the speakers.

The large freeform pool in the center was surrounded by a multitude of lounge chairs and cabanas, with lush green palms swaying in the breeze. A gentle lazy river curled around the perimeter, with soothing hot tubs dotting its path. Bright umbrellas and flowerbeds popped with color as the clean smell of chlorinated water and the sweet scent of frangipani and jasmine drifted through the air.

I frowned at the hot tubs.

Why anyone who spent more than three seconds in the Florida heat would want a hot tub was beyond me.

I spotted a few people from the rehearsal dinner in the crowd and waved as we approached chaise lounges beneath a patch of trees, providing some relief from the sun.

A woman in a pink dress and wide-brimmed hat waved and called out my name with her face lit up in recognition. A man nearby with a bald spot on his head shouted a hearty hello, too. I called back friendly greetings even though I couldn't remember their names.

Another woman I didn't recognize waved enthusiastically from under a large umbrella. "Astra! Hey, Astra! Hi, Astra!"

I offered a smile and waved back, then glanced at Lothian. "Do I know her?"

He shrugged. "No idea. Lots of Emma and Eddie's friends and extended family are here for the wedding. I don't remember most of them, either." The muscled werewolf looked at the clear blue sky and the unrelenting Florida sun. "The only thing I'm completely sure of is that none of them are vampires."

We spread out two large, striped beach towels over two lounge chairs, and I arranged myself on top of one. The sun's warmth radiated through the leaves of a nearby palm tree, sending a pattern of light and shadow across my bare skin.

"So that's a lazy river going around the perimeter?" I asked.

Lothian nodded. "Yep, and looks like they have a few hot tubs over there too. I love hot tubs."

He would.

"Why would anyone need a hot tub in Florida?" I asked, this time out loud.

He chuckled. "It's the perfect way to relax and release all the tension that builds up during the day, the day's stress just melting away. You should try it. You might like it. You'll feel so relaxed and content—"

"And sweaty and hot. No thanks." I rolled my eyes. "Crazy."

Our server approached with a tray of watermelon margaritas and gracefully placed them in front of us. Lothian accepted one of the frosty, fruity drinks, and as soon as the waiter left us, I glanced around the pool area, my eyes skimming past vague acquaintances and strangers alike. The drink was cool against my fingers, and I traced the rim distractedly while people-watching.

"See any likely suspects? Persons of interest?" Lothian asked, lowering his voice.

I shook my head. "Not yet. But give me time.

It's early."

I glanced at the hot tub and noticed an attractive woman in her fifties studying Lothian intently. Her glare was almost predatory as she licked her lips and shifted slightly in the steaming water, her gaze never leaving him.

Gross.

I caught his gaze and shifted my eyes toward her direction. I motioned toward her, making sure no one but Lothian saw. "I think you've been targeted," I smirked. "You know what they say about flies, honey, and vinegar."

Lothian laughed. "Actually, I don't. What do they say?"

"You catch more flies with honey than vinegar. Meaning, friendly chatter will yield more useful information than direct interrogation." I looked at him. "You've really never heard that?"

"No, I have. I just like hearing you talk." Lothian stretched out on his towel, hands behind his head. "Well then, chat away, honeybee. I'll just hang out, soak in the ambiance and take notes on your techniques."

"While in the hot tub, no doubt," I said under my breath.

Lothian's eyebrows shot up in amusement.

"Are you concerned I might hop in that hot tub, Astra?"

"Hardly." I tossed my hair over my shoulder and looked down at Lothian. The humid breeze felt heavy on my skin, and a bead of sweat trickled down my arm. "I just think they're ridiculous in this climate." I didn't specify whether the thing I thought was ridiculous was the hot tub or the cougar.

Lothian's mouth stretched into a knowing smile, and I quickly looked away, desperately trying to ignore the heat creeping up my neck. The werewolf was far too perceptive for his own good.

And mine.

I took a deep breath, gathering my wits. The day was early, and there was a murder to solve. Personal matters, and confusing werewolves, would have to wait.

For now, it was time to catch some flies.

Just as I swung my legs off the lounge, a voice called my name. It was a familiar voice, one I had not heard in a while.

"Astra. I'd hoped to see you."

I looked up to find a male form that form radiated power and intensity, physical features perfectly sculpted and oddly ageless. He was tall and muscular, with a powerful jawline and features that could have been chiseled from marble. The sunlight seemed to emanate from his very being, surrounding him in a glow of golden light.

I locked eyes with a man who's gaze could see straight into the depths of one's soul, his eyes gleaming with heavenly enlightenment and insight—my father, the Greek god Apollo. "Hi, Dad."

# CHAPTER NINE

othian, the bootlicking toady, immediately sprang to his bare feet and eagerly grasped Apollo's hand. "Lykeios, what an immense honor this is, sir!" he gushed, his eyes alight with reverence as he pumped Apollo's arm up and down. "It is a pleasure to see you, sir. Truly."

I rolled my eyes.

The name the werewolf called my dad—Lykeios—was one of my father's many names, and it meant "of the wolf." Maybe I wasn't being entirely fair to Lothian when I called him a bootlicking toady. Honestly, the werewolf and the god had a mythical bond I wasn't a part of and, frankly, didn't understand.

The old stories say that when my grandmother Leto was pregnant with my father Apollo and Aunt Artemis, Hera was jealous and tried to stop her from having them. But Leto managed to get to the floating island of Delos, where some wolves protected her from Hera's schemes so she could give birth. Some people think those same wolves helped my dad pick the spot for his oracle at Delphi.

So, yeah. Dad and wolves.

Long history.

Apollo grasped his hand firmly. "Here in Forkbridge, I'm just Dr. Loxias, Lothian. But thank you." His piercing gaze flicked to me. "Astra. It's good to see you."

I took in my father's figure, noting the toned arms and broad chest. There was only a hint of gray at his temples, and I was struck by how much he had changed since we'd first met in Palm Beach. "You're looking...different."

"Handsome, I hope."

These two guys were seriously going to make my eyeballs fall out of my head with all the eye-rolling they caused. "Sure, Dad. You look good."

"Thank you, even though that seemed very insincere." Dr. Loxias shrugged, a smile playing at the corners of his mouth. "I'm single again. A man has to put his best foot forward."

"Why are you here?"

"I'm performing the wedding ceremony." Dr. Loxias clasped his hands behind his back. "Surely Emma mentioned I was coming?"

Um.

No.

"She did not mention that you were performing the wedding ceremony, no." I grabbed my watermelon margarita and took a big gulp. Of course, Emma didn't give me a heads up that my dear old dad would be here. And she should have. She knew how I felt about the idea of my father. I had issues with him, and that's putting it mildly.

Dr. Loxias sighed. "I had hoped this weekend might be an opportunity for us to reconnect a bit."

Reconnect?

That implied an initial connection we didn't have.

"When are we going to have the time?" I sipped my margarita as he chuckled, the sound as rich and melodic as I remembered. "When you're performing the ceremony, and I'm the maid of honor? I doubt there's going to be much time for us to sit and talk, Dad."

"We're sitting and talking now, daughter."

"You're standing."

"You're still angry with me." It wasn't a question. Dr. Loxias moved to sit on my lounge chair, his oddly golden eyes searching my face. "I understand. But avoiding each other won't undo the past. I hoped that in time, you might come around."

He hoped I might come around.

In time.

Time didn't heal all wounds, not where the gods were concerned.

Or where witches were concerned.

Or where fathers and daughters were concerned.

I took another sip of my drink.

The day suddenly felt heavier, the sun hotter. I prayed for a downpour to send all these wedding guests scrambling inside and cut this little father-daughter reunion short. "Actually, Lothian and I were hoping to get some investigating done today. Did Emma tell you her Uncle Albert died last night?" – "My condolences to Emma—mortal lives end so fleetingly." Dr. Loxias nodded, unsurprised. "But yes, I did know. You're staying in the dead man's hotel room." He glanced at Lothian. "With him." My father paused dramatically as his brow furrowed and then added, "The room only has one large bed."

"Oh, we are not doing that," I said under my breath. "I'm not a child. You don't get a say in where I sleep or who I sleep with."

Dr. Loxias peered at me with those piercing golden eyes that seemed to see right into my soul and then raised an eyebrow. "I'm well aware of that. However, as a god of order, purity, and moderation, I generally frown upon excessive or uncontrolled sexuality. I'd be remiss if I didn't speak up and say something when—"

I let out a humorless laugh. "Says the god who was notorious for his affairs. You didn't exactly practice what you just preached to me about chastity." – He smiled. "True, my private life as a god can be...complicated. But as your father, I wish to see you make sound choices, that's all" His golden gaze slid to Lothian. "Ones that don't end in heartbreak."

My jaw clenched.

I didn't need immortal life advice from the god who'd been absent nearly all of mine. "Thanks for the concern, but I've been doing just fine making my own choices."

Apollo looked unconvinced but, thankfully, let it drop.

Then he sighed and said, "You're angry. It continues to amaze me that so much of humanity still calls on me for help, and yet I don't seem to be able to take a step in any direction but backward with you. We have the chance to move past your anger if you take it."

I took a long drink of my margarita.

Yep, today was definitely going to call for more of these.

I gazed at the pool without really seeing it, my mind swirling with memories that came with way too much emotional baggage to deal with right now. Maybe not ever.

The truth was, I didn't know if I could ever truly move on from it. The fact that Apollo chose not to tell me who he really was when we first met still infuriated me. It formed the basis of the distrust at the core of our relationship. He had literal ages to become a better god and a better person, but he couldn't be bothered.

I only had a single mortal lifetime to get over the pain his actions had caused.

To have a parent casually waltz into your life whenever they pleased without warning or apology, or honesty?

No matter how much Apollo insisted he cared or wanted us to be closer, his actions proved otherwise. You don't hide the truth about who you are from someone while asking for their love and trust.

You just don't.

I would not be another toy in another god's celestial games.

I put down my half-full margarita with a clunk. "Let's just focus on why we're both really here this weekend—for Emma and Eddie." I stood up and brushed off imaginary dirt from my thighs. "If you'll excuse me, I need another drink."

Before "Dr. Loxias" could respond, I walked off toward the poolside bar without looking back. I couldn't deal with Apollo's manipulations or make any promises about reconnecting. Not this weekend.

Not yet.

Maybe not ever.

For now, there was a wedding to attend and a murder to solve, and that was enough to focus on.

The rest of my life would have to wait.

* * *

I SLID onto an open barstool at the pool bar, my eyes scanning for the bartender. He was occupied polishing a glass with his white towel. I conspicuously cleared my throat until he glanced over, then said, "Dirty martini, extra olives."

The bartender raised his eyebrows at that but wisely chose not to comment.

He set to making my drink, grabbing the vodka and vermouth bottles with a practiced flourish. Within moments, an icy cold glass was being pushed across the bar toward me. I muttered thanks and took a greedy gulp of the martini.

A few more of these drinks, and maybe I'd be able to get through the rest of this infernal wedding party without accidentally incinerating someone with a star-power-infused glare and point.

Today definitely qualified as a "whatever it takes" kind of day.

The woman on the stool next to mine gave me an approving nod. "Good choice. Looks like you could use a strong drink after that tense conversation with those two hotties." She raised her arm languidly and gestured toward the lounges where my father and Lothian were still seated, deep in conversation. "Those two giving you trouble?"

Not only had the booze numbed my emotional ache and anger, but it had also apparently dulled my senses, too, because Emma's cousin Beatrice perched on a stool next to me.

"They're fine," I responded.

"They sure are," she laughed. Beatrice was wearing a hot pink bikini that hugged her curves, her almost white blond hair (no doubt from a bottle) cascading down her sin-kissed shoulders. She glanced at me coyly from underneath heavily mascaraed lashes. "If you need some help, I'll be happy to take one off your hands. I'll even let you pick."

"You're welcome to the long-haired one," I told her, gesturing toward the werewolf. "In fact, if you managed to get him away from the pool, you'd help me out." I avoided mentioning my father or how I knew either of the men but pushed Lothian as an option in hopes that he could spend some alone time with her and get us information.

"Of course. I'm happy to offer my services." Beatrice grinned, showing off teeth bleached to an almost neon white. "I'm Beatrice, by the way. Emma's cousin."

"Astra. Maid of Honor. Nice to meet you." I took another sip. The chilled gin slid down my throat, and I savored the tangy burst of olive brine and herbs.

"Hey, Astra. Nice to meet you."

"Uh-huh." I wasn't normally a drinker, but I was starting to understand why weddings had a reputation for being a hotbed of drunken relatives steeped in alcohol. The voices and laughter echoing around the pool were beginning to sound pleasantly muffled and distant. "You and I met last night, actually."

Beatrice pouted. "We did? I don't remember. My memory isn't the best, I'm afraid. Probably from one too many wild nights." She let out an exaggerated sigh. "The curse of being young and beautiful. Too many parties, not enough rest."

The bartender stepped away to help another guest—but not before giving me a pointed look that said he expected he'd be seeing a lot more of me.

I gritted my teeth and met Beatrice's eyes, searching for some sign of maturity in her bright green gaze. We looked to be the same age, or close to it, but her demeanor was that of an immature twenty-something with no cares in the world. "Don't worry about it. We only met briefly at the rehearsal dinner." I suppressed a sigh and forced a polite smile.

If I had my choice, this exchange would have ended right there, and that would be the extent of our acquaintance… but it wasn't my choice. I was here to focus on Albert's murder—and my very first suspect was Emma's vapid cousin.

As potential diabolical villains went, this woman didn't exactly fit the profile. She looked about as threatening as a rum-soaked marshmallow.

Beatrice's lips pursed into a pout as she picked up her glass off the bar top. "Oh, well, no matter. We're meeting again now!" Rolling her shoulders in a seductive sway, she sauntered across the pool deck with her hips swaying with purpose and determination. She stopped to grin wickedly over her shoulder at me. "Come on, we don't want anyone to take those hot boys!"

My stomach lurched at her words as I fought to keep the boozy contents of my empty stomach down. I swallowed hard and followed Beatrice across the pool deck, my martini clutched in one hand.

This was an opportunity, I told myself, despite the churning in my gut.

If Beatrice was truly as vapid and self-centered as she seemed, she might let something slip while distracted.

As soon as we reached my father and Lothian, Beatrice began shamelessly flirting with the werewolf. She leaned into his personal space, twirling a lock of hair around one finger and contorting herself so she could gaze down at him through lowered lashes. "Your name is Lothian. How exotic! Astra told me you're looking for a date, hot stuff."

Lothian's mouth widened into a smirk, and his blue eyes twinkled with feigned delight as he locked gazes with Beatrice. "Did she, now? A pleasure to make your acquaintance." His gaze quickly darted toward me, and I could see a flash of anger on his face for an instant before he shifted his attention back to her.

He'll get over it, I thought.

Dr. Loxias narrowed his bushy eyebrows together in a fierce frown. "It's so sad to see how little appreciation is given to the virtues of restraint and moderation. Every journey should be undertaken cautiously, don't you agree?"

I fought to keep a straight face.

That was my dear old dad's roundabout, passive-aggressive way of saying Beatrice's dramatics were getting on his last divine nerve. Subtlety and indirectness were qualities Apollo prided himself on, and his snide little comment just now proved Beatrice's flair for the over the top had worn through even his patience—infinite as it supposedly was. When gods actually came right out and said what they thought directly and without mincing words, you were usually already toast.

Beatrice sighed dramatically, slipping one arm around Lothian's bicep. "You're so right, Dr. Loxias. Moderation is a virtue people just don't appreciate anymore. I just lost my dear Uncle Albert last night, and you might say it was all because he just wasn't a cautious man. A girl sure could use some comfort at a time like this." Her eyes roamed over Lothian's body. "And you look like you'd be very... comforting."

Ew.

I felt my skin crawl as nausea began to take hold again... but she had brought up the dead uncle.

It was the perfect opportunity to get her talking.

"I'm so sorry to hear about your uncle,

Beatrice," I said. "How are you holding up?" – She shrugged, her arms still wrapped tightly around Lothian. "Uncle Albert lived a good, long life, but it's never easy to let go." Her voice caught, and she took a deep breath.

"Were you close with your uncle?"

Beatrice wrinkled her nose. "Not particularly. Well, we were once in a while, but not so much lately. We had a bit of a falling out recently, to be honest. But family is family." She drunkenly snuggled into the warm crook of Lothian's neck and inhaled his scent with a loud snort. He shot me a desperate glance above her head. "At least I have big strong arms to comfort me now. Don't I, Loth?"

Lothian winced.

Dad cleared his throat. "I'm afraid I must take my leave. Wedding duties call." He eyed Beatrice with thinly veiled disapproval. "Do exercise some restraint, young lady, won't you?"

Wow. That was pretty direct.

Eyes twinkling mischievously, Beatrice bit her lip and suppressed a giggle as a sly smirk crossed her face. "Oh, yeah," she replied eagerly, "I will. I love restraints." Her lasciviousness leer made it clear that she and my father were definitely not talking about the same thing.

With another frown and a nod to Lothian and me, Dad turned on his heel and strode off across toward the pool gate.

I sighed, wishing I could make my own hasty exit.

But there were still questions to ask, and Beatrice seemed willing to talk, even if her target audience appeared to be Lothian's biceps.

# CHAPTER TEN

*I* watched Beatrice closely, taking in her disheveled hot mess of an appearance. It was obvious she had been drinking for a while already, even though it was barely past morning. She hiccuped loudly, then brought a shaky hand to her mouth as she giggled. "Oh my, excuse me!" her voice rang out, too loud and too shrill.

"No problem," I mumbled.

Beatrice's gaze wandered around the pool, her eyes dull and listless. She slumped against Lothian for support, her limbs as limp as a rag doll's as she blabbered on without thinking, her voice shooting up with each drunken giggle.

This was my chance.

With the woman wasted and not paying

attention to the words coming out of her mouth, she might let something slip about her uncle's death, I thought. Then I pounced like a cheetah chasing a tipsy gazelle.

"Did Albert have any health problems?"

Bea turned to me in slow motion, eyes struggling to focus, and blinked. "I guess. Old folks always do." She erupted into a fit of shrill laughter as if she'd told an unintentional joke.

"Was he on any meds?"

"Beats me. We weren't close." She hiccuped again. "Ask his nurse or doctor or whatever. One of them. They'd know more than me. I don't know anything."

"No? Did you not talk to your uncle recently?"

"Nah. We had a fight, remember?" Beatrice took another gulp of her drink, her alcohol-infused mind visibly struggling to piece details together as she swayed in her seat. "Over money or something. Might've been about the will." She looked up at the sky. "Was it the will? Huh. I dunno. Can't remember what exactly now. I mean, he's dead. Doesn't matter anymore." Bea took another long sip of her drink before erupting into a fit of hysterical laughter; the remaining liquid threatened to splash out as her unsteady hand vibrated.

Lothian sat next to her rigidly, his eyes SOS signals of distress firing off in my direction as the drunk cousin clung to his arm like a remora attached to an ocean-going shark. She'd looped her own arm through his, her fingers clutching the fabric of his swim shorts as if to ensure he couldn't accidentally slip away. The discomfort was written all over his face.

"Do you know if your uncle left you anything in his will?" I asked.

Beatrice waved her hand, nearly toppling her glass. "The lawyers will figure all that out. I don't concern myself with stuff like that. What do I care?" She nuzzled into Lothian's shoulder and sloppily planted a big wet kiss somewhere in the neighborhood of his armpit. "All I need to concern myself with is big strong arms like these!"

I frowned.

Last night she cared.

The night before, Beatrice had absolutely concerned herself with such matters, raging about inheritance disputes and unfairness—but that, of course, was before Albert's death. Now she was sloshing down drinks without a care as if she didn't give two figs he was dead.

Talk about mood swings.

The vitriol and hysterics from only twenty-four hours ago seemed too focused to just shrug off overnight, intoxicated or not.

Either Beatrice was drunk enough to forget she'd cared pretty deeply just last night, or she was just sober enough to put on a convincing act that none of it mattered to her despite previous words and appearances.

"You should slow down on the booze, Beatrice," Lothian said gently, trying to squirm out of her grip. "Wouldn't want you getting sick at the big family bash."

Beatrice pouted. "You're such a buzzkill. I'm here to party!" She let out a loud hiccup, then burst into giggles. "Guess I already went overboard. Whoops!" With an exaggerated sigh, she stumbled off the chaise lounge and held out her hand to the werewolf. "Time for a nap. Wanna come up to my room and cuddle?"

"Uh, no, I believe Astra and I have—"

"Buzzkill!" Beatrice shrieked, waving her hand at Lothian in dismissal. "Call me if you get lonely, Loth!" She spun on her heel and stumbled across the deck, bouncing off chairs and bewildered guests like a pinball. Partygoers gasped and dodged out of her way as she careened past.

"Thank the gods, I didn't think she'd ever leave." Lothian shot an accusing frown at me. "How about a head's up the next time before throwing me into the lion's den?" He swiped an exhausted hand down his face. "I could have used a bit of warning that you were going to use me as bait."

"Bait? Hardly. You didn't get jack from her. And when you had the chance to get her alone up in some hotel room, you let her walk away. If I'd worked my magic, I'd have gotten way more out of this than you." I glared. "You didn't even take advantage of your in with her."

"Are you kidding me?" Lothian's eyes flashed as he glared at me. "She's totally wasted! Did you really think I'd follow her upstairs when she's that drunk?" He glared at me, obviously angry. "I can't believe you'd suggest that. There are lines I won't cross, Astra. And this? This was one of them."

"Lines you won't cross?" I snorted. "Who're you kidding? I just grilled her with questions to take advantage of how weak she is. You couldn't tuck her into bed at her invitation to get a little more information?"

Lothian gazed down the garden path where Beatrice had disappeared. "I can't believe you'd even suggest that." He turned back and looked at me. "That's totally different."

"How's that different?"

He looked away once more. "We were in public, and it was just talking. She wanted to drag me into her hotel room, just the two of us, and she wanted... more than talk." Lothian's eyes flashed, angry, and he turned to face me. "It's different, and you know it," he snapped.

I met his furious glare calmly. "Fine, it's different," I replied evenly. "I'm also sure it's something you've done before, so I don't know why you're getting all high and mighty about doing it now."

Lothian's eyes widened, his mouth falling open as if I had struck him, and the tension between us was thick. Without a word, he stood up fast, spun around, and stormed off across the courtyard.

The path swallowed him up as he vanished into the dense trees around the pool.

Damn it.

* * *

I SAT AT THE POOLSIDE, swirling what was left of my martini as I watched the other guests enjoying themselves. Despite the heat, I felt chilled. A knot of guilt had settled in my stomach, even though I hadn't actually done anything wrong.

Had I?

Lothian getting all bent out of shape left me confused. Everything about the guy, from the fancy suits to the smooth moves, screamed player. Bet he'd broken hearts and talked more than a few not-so-willing ladies into giving him what he wanted. I was sure of it. Heck, when I met him, he more or less claimed he had. Proudly.

But imply he's got a manipulative side, and boom—dude blows a gasket.

You insulted his honor, a little voice whispered. Questioned his ethics and boundaries.

I frowned, staring into the briny depths of my drink.

Maybe I had misjudged the werewolf.

I mean, his reaction certainly indicated I'd struck a nerve by implying he'd take advantage of an intoxicated woman to get information. Maybe despite coming off like some smooth player, he draws the line at messing with someone totally wasted. Maybe that kinda thing didn't sit right with him, and he didn't like me suggesting it.

Did you really think he'd do that? the voice asked. Or were you just lashing out in anger?

Anger? Hardly, I told the voice in my head.

I probably just bruised his delicate ego. Lothian sees himself as a ladies' man, and my implication that he'd have to resort to shady moves with a drunk chick to score wounded his pride, that's all. Cue the outrage.

I sighed, rubbing my temples.

I watched a couple splash and laugh together in the pool, envying their carefree joy. It must be nice to be so blissfully oblivious and happy-go-lucky. It was a state I could never remember being in.

Not once.

I sighed, dragging my morose gaze from the frolicking couple to stare moodily at Lothian's abandoned fruity cocktail as if it held the solutions to all my problems. The little paper umbrella floating in his drink seemed to mock me. I had about as much chance of relaxation and enjoyment in life as that silly paper prop had of actually shielding someone from an afternoon thunderstorm.

The guests frolicking poolside suddenly jumped in unison at the hair-raising screech of an owl far too close to the pool for anyone's comfort.

Well, that's what they heard.

That's not what I heard.

I heard Archie instead, yelling, "Hey, clueless!" in his usual annoyed tone as he perched on the fence surrounding the pool.

While the oblivious sunbathers cowered in fear at the angry owl in their midst, Archie took no notice and continued shrieking up a storm in words only I could discern.

"You really work at ignoring that voice in the back of your head, don't you?" Archie asked shrilly from across the pool deck. "These fools don't even know what I'm saying, and they know to pay attention to me. You? You ignore your voice in your head, my voice in your head, your father's voice outside your head, your sister's—"

I rose from the poolside chaise. "I'm going back to my room," I said, my voice ringing louder than intended across the patio.

The guests looked at me, then gradually relaxed as the lack of follow-up calls or attacks from the feathered predator eased their fears. It didn't take long for the poolside revelry to return to its previous volume—and just like that, Archie was forgotten amid laughter and resumed splash fights.

People really did have the memory of goldfish.

I gathered my things and walked down one of the winding pathways leading away from the pool, the dense foliage closing in around me. The chatter and screams of delight faded, replaced by the rustle of palm fronds overhead and the calls of unfamiliar birds.

It was peaceful here in—

"You need to stop being so defensive and try enjoying yourself for once!" Archie flitted between the treetops above, hopping from branch to branch as he resumed his judgmental tirade. "Set aside all that emotional baggage about Jason and live a little for once, will ya? Your best friend is getting married. To a werewolf! She's marrying into the paranormal world! Her kid is in the paranormal world! Are you helping her through that? No. No, of course not. Honestly, I wonder sometimes what Athena was thinking choosing you, that stick up your—"

"All right, that's enough! There was a murder at my best friend's rehearsal dinner, remember?" I snapped, stomping down the path. My patience for lectures from immortal Greek beings with an overinflated sense of their wisdom was at an end for the day, and it wasn't even lunchtime. "It's kind of hard to relax with a murderer on the loose."

"Does it look like anyone else gives two hoots about that poor sod Albert?" Archie ruffled his feathers. "Literally! Look around! Nobody cares! The man's dead, Astra. Let the local cops worry about it and have some fun for once in your life!"

I scowled up at the owl. "I work for the local cops, featherbrain. And last I checked, cold-blooded murder tends to ruin most people's idea of fun."

"You work where?" Archie stared down at me. "You were fired because Daniel's playing hide the salami with Jason's mother, and that woman can't get over what happened any more than you can! Emma hasn't gone back to work since the baby was born. Has there been some change in employment for you or her that I'm unaware of?"

What I wouldn't give for a beak-shaped muzzle.

I started walking again, and the path opened up into a tiny waypoint courtyard filled with exotic blooms around a stone bench. Their sweet fragrance mingled with the loamy scent of damp foliage, and I brushed past a drooping cluster of orchids without stopping.

"You love orchids." Archie's words fell hard as stones, his voice laced with unspoken recrimination.

The floral aroma that had seemed pleasant moments before now cloyed and suffocated. "Go away, Archie. I don't need you passing judgment on my decision to walk by a flower."

Archie swooped down ahead of me, landing on the carved stone bench beneath a curtain of pink flowers. He peered at me and blinked dramatically. "You're stuck in the past again, dwelling on things you can't change. Jason's gone. He's off having his best death with a girl that suits him better than you ever did. Nothing you do will bring him back. But everything you're doing might push everybody still here away from you. Including that werewolf you can't stop having dreams about."

My pace slowed, anger and grief warring for dominance inside me. My eyes stung, but I refused to shed any tears over this again, especially not in front of Archie. Not when he was like this.

"Why can't you just—"

"You think I don't know Jason's gone?" I asked in a low voice. "You don't understand. I'm not trying to bring Jason back. This has nothing to do with Jason or Lothian. I'm trying to get justice for Albert and keep his murder from ruining Emma's wedding. That's all. Stop reading into everything I do."

"Justice?" Archie ruffled his feathers again, annoyed. "Don't give me that. This isn't about justice, and we both know it. It's about your guilt. Your refusal to accept what happened and move on with your life. You're using this belief that Albert was murdered to keep yourself isolated from the wedding, from Emma, from—"

"Stop it." I swallowed hard against the sudden lump in my throat. Archie's words struck deep, reopening barely-healed wounds I fought to ignore, and I didn't want to examine my motivations or the turmoil of emotions his prodding stirred up. I just wanted to get through this stupid wedding weekend and solve this murder without picking apart my own messy feelings. Was that too much to ask?

"Stop what?"

"You think you know everything." I avoided Archie's gaze, staring at the pink flowers and vibrant green leaves instead. "But you don't. Just fly off and pester someone else. Before I clip your wings to keep you at home where you're supposed to be."

"So that's how it's going to be, is it?" Archie let out an irritated hoot. "I swear, woman, you're impossible!" He took off in a flurry of rustling foliage, vanishing into the sky with another "Impossible! Just impossible!" that sounded to everyone else like several mighty shrieks of fury.

I let out a shaky breath and continued down the path leading to my room, determined not to dwell on the argument with Archie or Lothian's anger.

* * *

LOST IN THOUGHT, I wandered down the garden path until a figure emerged from the shadows ahead. I gasped, narrowly avoiding collision with the man's wiry frame.

He stood a head taller than me, all sharp angles and edges. Stringy black hair hung to his shoulders, framing an angular face. His feeble attempt at a beard did little to offset a receding chin and washed-out complexion that screamed lack of sunlight.

Victor De Luca smiled at me.

A chill slithered down my spine as I gazed up at this ominous stranger. In an instant, every instinct suddenly screamed at me to turn heel and flee that grinning facade hinting at the menace beneath.

"Oh, excuse me," I said, attempting to sidestep him.

Vincent held up his hands. "No trouble. My fault. I should've been watching where I was going." His gaze traveled the length of me slowly, and then he smiled even more widely. "I know you. You're the town psychic, the one that worked with Connie's cousin Emma." Every forced, hollow smile and exaggerated laugh felt calculated to set me at ease and hide his sharp, restless scrutiny. He raised his eyebrow. "You in a hurry?"

"I am both that psychic and in a hurry. You're the DJ, right? Nice to meet you. Anyway, if you'll excuse me, I was just heading to my room." I forced a polite smile, keenly aware we were alone on this secluded path and looked pointedly at the path behind him. My fingers tightened around the strap of my bag, senses on high alert.

"I'm a radio talk show host, not a DJ," Vincent said, ignoring my desire to leave. He cocked his head and stared at me with an intensity that set my teeth on edge. "I couldn't help overhearing... were you arguing with a bird a moment ago?"

I let out a strained laugh. "Arguing with a

bird? Actually, come to think of it, I could make big money on the internet filming arguments with birds. All the rage these days, right? I love those blue chicken videos. Anyway, if you'll excuse me—"

"Interesting." His eyes narrowed a fraction. "You didn't answer my question."

You'd think after encouraging Lothian to fake a whirlwind wedding weekend romance with the sloppy lush Beatrice, I'd be eager to use Victor's more than obvious interest in me to get the intel I needed.

You'd think.

But you'd be wrong.

Every alarm in my head was clanging just being near Victor. Something was way, way off about this guy—my instincts were screaming that I needed to be anywhere else right now except alone with him on this isolated path.

"No, I didn't answer your question." The smile slid from my face. "It's not really any of your business who I was talking to, though, is it? For the last time, I'd like to leave and get back to my room. Have a good afternoon."

I moved to sidestep around him, but Vincent swayed into my path. Though he uttered not a word, his intent rang loud in the space between us, the amused grin remaining plastered on his face. His focus rested solely on me.

This wasn't the first time he'd done something like this, I thought to myself. He was too smooth at it, too comfortable with the menacing game.

Sleazeball.

I will admit that part of me was scolding myself for passing up such an easy opportunity. He was practically rolling out the red carpet for me to spend time with him, even if his ultimate intentions were... questionable.

My self-preservation instincts, on the other hand, were giving me a firm "Run, don't walk, away from this creep!" message on repeat. The hairs on the back of my neck stood at attention under Victor's unsettling gaze.

I knew that look.

I'd looked at people the same way before when I was in the military.

Those eyes were probing for a weakness to exploit.

"Now, now, no need to get testy," Vincent said. "I was just curious, that's all. These old resorts often have interesting and unique wildlife." He studied me with that piercing gaze as if trying to see inside my mind. "Although your... conversation... sounded rather one-sided. Unless the local birds have learned to talk back?" A sly grin spread across his face. "Maybe you have other gifts, like that doctor who talks to animals."

I squared my shoulders and met his gaze steadily. "I don't have any special gifts besides the ones everyone knows about. Now if you'll excuse me, I have somewhere to be." I brushed past him forcefully without waiting for a response, my heart pounding as I hurried down the path. I hoped he would give way and not stand firm or reach out to stop me. I didn't want to have to sizzle-fry a wedding guest among the palm fronds.

He didn't stop me.

This was more than his interest in the local psychic that worked with the police and found a missing puppy, I thought as I hurried away. Beneath the veneer of attempted flirtation lurked something predatory, cold, and cunning.

Those probing eyes were evaluating me, weighing options like a hunter gauging its prey.

# CHAPTER ELEVEN

*I* flung open the door to my hotel room and stomped inside, dropping my bag on the floor with a thud. The anger from my encounter with Victor still pulsed through me, but I was relieved to be back in the quiet isolation of the hotel room. I was in no mood for any more lectures or judgment or confrontation today—

I blinked, my feeling of refuge evaporating in an instant as six eyes stared back at me.

Archie perched on the back of one of the chairs. Lothian sat on the little sofa, his face about as easy to read as ancient Sanskrit. Over by the sliding glass doors leading to the balcony, my father stood tucked into a corner, staring back at me with a smug smile. Before I could speak, my dad stepped to reveal the floor-length mirror behind him.

Eight eyes.

Not six.

Eight eyes.

There, in the luminescent blue mirror by the side of the sliding glass door, was Jason's familiar ethereal face staring back at me. His glowy azure image, situated across the room from me, threw me that same cheeky smile that I had come to know so intimately.

Well.

Glad the dead guy was happy.

"Hey, Astra," Jason said.

My gaze bounced between Archie's poker face, Apollo's half-grin, Jason's inscrutable shimmering eyes, and Lothian's obvious unease.

I wanted to punch every one of them in the face.

I inhaled harshly and got a snootful of Lothian's familiar sandalwood scent mixed with my father's aroma of amber and laurel—warm, faintly spicy, slightly sweet. The heady fragrance designed to calm caused the apprehension and anger to swell in me.

"Hello, Jason. I didn't realize you were invited to

the wedding, too." My voice came out steady despite the maelstrom of rage inside. I folded my arms tight and braced myself for whatever these four men had up their sleeves. "What did I just walk into here?" I glanced at Apollo again. "An intervention?"

Jason's grin faded. "Not exactly."

"That's not a bad word for it, actually." Apollo disagreed and then cleared his throat. "Your friends and family are concerned for you, Astra. This has gone on long enough."

"What, exactly, is it that has gone on long enough? Your curse on Cassandra? King Midas' donkey ears? Daphne hiding from you in a forest? Do you even remember which tree she is? You know, now that I think about it, is it me, or do your love stories always end up in heartbreak and catastrophe?"

My father's face didn't so much as ripple. "Astra—"

"Wait a second. I have one more. Isn't it convenient to be the god of truth when you are the one who decides what truth is?" I glared at Archie. "Did you do this?"

The owl hooted. "Hey now, don't give me that look. I'm just here. Moral support and all that, right?"

"Who's moral support are we talking about here? Mine or theirs?"

He shuffled on his perch and averted his gaze, pretending to be suddenly fascinated by a knot in the wood.

"Archie?"

Without looking at me, he shifted his attention to preening his feathers.

Lothian rose from the sofa, his expression grim. "Look, I know this seems like it's a bit over the top, but we are worried you're getting a little obsessed with investigating Albert's death—"

"—to avoid dealing with other things," my father interjected.

"No," Lothian retorted, eyes flashing as he fixed Apollo with a steely gaze. "No, that's not what I said." He finished his words in a rush, running a hand through his hair in frustration. "I just... look, you haven't been yourself this weekend, and before this goes any further, we all just thought—"

My eyes felt hot. It was as if there was a firestorm within them ignited by his words. "Before this goes any further, how about you just back off?"

"Astra..." His voice trailed off, unfinished, hanging in the tension-charged air between us.

His eyes softened for a moment as he glanced away, his hands gesturing vaguely in the air as if to summon the right words.

"No. Just because I'm trying to solve a murder instead of guzzling fruity cocktails by the pool does not mean I have 'issues.' Honestly, the four of you have a hell of a lot of nerve cornering me in my own hotel room as if you know better than what's in my head."

"This is Albert's hotel room," Archie pointed out.

"You were supposed to be home with your sisters," Apollo added.

"No, Archie was supposed to be home with my sisters," I snapped.

"Astra, believe it or not, everyone here cares about you." Jason's eyes held mine from across the room. "But I have to agree with your father. It seems like you're using this investigation like a shield to hide from the emotions Emma's wedding is bringing up in you."

I shook my head. "You're wrong."

"You threatened to clip Archie's wings. You've been drinking more than I've ever seen you drink. And as for what you said to the werewolf —I know you don't really think Lothian goes around taking advantage of women." Jason watched me, his eyes pools of still water reflecting the softness of his smile.

"I..." I didn't know what to say. Having it all laid out like that? Yeah, it seemed like I was being a little harsh this weekend.

"Well, do you really believe that?" There was nothing demanding or impatient in Jason's tone, but I found it hard to answer under Lothian's gaze.

I swallowed hard. "Look, I'm just trying to do my job and find justice for—"

"Your job for who, exactly, daughter?" Apollo arched one eyebrow. "You don't work for the police any longer. There's no need for you to solve Albert's death. Athena has not charged you to protect him or anyone else this weekend. The authorities will handle the investigation. It's not your job at all. Your job is to be a maid of honor to your friend."

My father's smug condescension was infuriating, and I knew if I answered, I was going to tear him a new one.

So I stood, silent.

A long beat ticked by, filled with the sounds of us breathing and the shrieks of laughter drifting up from downstairs. Then Archie dragged his talon against the chair, and I winced at the nails-on-chalkboard scrape.

I was so angry.

So angry.

This was infuriating and humiliating.

My hands sparked as I itched to rip into the whole lot of them and point out that I was a grown woman being cornered by a pack of Neanderthals who thought they needed to "handle" me and my emotional issues. It infuriated me, and I wondered how long it would take for someone to say I was being too emotional.

My fingers twitched at my sides, itching to ball into fists. I wanted nothing more than to wind up and slug each of them in their too-handsome faces.

Even Lothian… Okay, well, maybe not Lothian. His discomfort was palpable, and I could almost taste the bitter tang of regret and awkwardness rolling off him. He probably hadn't asked for this any more than I had.

But the rest of them.

There was one problem with that—if I exploded at them, they'd never go away.

Finally, I let out a long breath. "Look, I don't need an intervention, and I get what you're saying. And you're right. I've been a bit out of sorts, and I... appreciate your concern." I met each gaze in turn, my glare softening when it reached Lothian, anger melting into resignation. "However misguided."

Jason smiled gently. "Great. Now sit down. Let's talk about the murder."

I sighed, suddenly feeling very weary as I sank into an armchair.

* * *

THE RESIGNATION, to be honest, was nothing more than my realization that I'd have to make them feel they accomplished something in order to get them all out of my bedroom.

I was still fighting the urge to tell the lot of them where they could stick their unsolicited advice and opinions, and the only thing keeping me in that stupid chair was the previously mentioned knowledge that unleashing my temper (as deserved as it might have been) would only make the situation drag on longer.

"Look, I know you think I'm just 'making up' a murder to occupy myself, but I'm not." I took a deep breath and began laying out the details for them, and I tried not to feel like I was justifying myself to them. "Last night at the rehearsal dinner, I witnessed an argument between Albert and Beatrice. She was furious that he planned to leave the radio station to Vincent, not her. Soon after, Albert choked on a piece of quiche—but when I touched him, what I saw and experienced felt much more like an allergic reaction."

Apollo frowned. "An allergic reaction? But people saw him choke."

"I know what people think they saw, but the quiche thing is weird. Quiche is soft and easy to chew. It's recommended for people with trouble swallowing." I shrugged. "Then there's this place. When Lothian and I searched this room, it had been wiped clean. No suitcase, no clothes, nothing. It was like Albert had never been here, but we know he was. Where'd all Albert's stuff go?"

Jason's eyes narrowed. "Robbery?"

"Maybe, but his stuff disappeared awfully fast, and robbers don't generally clean up a room. Beatrice's reaction to Albert's death, too, was strange—last night she cared about inheritance, today she doesn't." I pressed my lips together. "Then there's Simon Kincaid. He has some health food store in Orlando but was giving Albert pills here in this room. And let's not forget super creepy Victor De Luca. He's dating another of Emma's cousins, Connie, but was…" I trailed off. "Let's just say he was oddly focused on me today."

"What do you mean?" Lothian frowned. "De Luca approached you? When?"

I described my encounter with Victor on the garden path, the probing questions and predatory interest that set my senses on alert. "He asked if I was arguing with a bird. And whether I have 'other gifts' besides psychometry." I looked at Archie. "He overheard us."

Archie shuffled on his perch. "Sorry. I should have been more discreet."

"You think this De Luca character is involved with Albert's death?" Apollo asked.

"I don't know. But to be honest, his interest in me seems more than casual, and the timing of him showing up here with one of Emma's cousins is suspicious. Not only that, I think she said she's a nurse." I leaned forward, linking my fingers. "Look, I know I'm not with the police anymore. But if Albert was murdered, I want to find out who did it and make sure nothing else happens at this wedding. I owe that much to Emma, at least."

Lothian perched at the edge of the sofa, forearms resting on jean-clad thighs as he bent forward. "You know I have some of the same suspicions as you, and I don't think you're making this up to avoid whatever they think you're trying to avoid." The werewolf's gaze slid to my father for a fleeting moment, his eyes glinting. "But you don't have enough evidence to say for sure this is a murder. It's all speculation." His gaze softened. "I know you want to help, but promise me you'll be careful. De Luca sounds dangerous, and if he's involved, poking around could put you at risk. Emma will kill me if I let something happen to you before the wedding."

After?

It would just be maiming.

The rebuttal formed on my lips, defiant, before fading away. As much as I hated to admit it, Lothian had a point. We had suspicions aplenty, but theories alone did not make a case. No indisputable evidence pointed to a single clear culprit, much less that it was a murder.

"You're right." My anger drained away, leaving frustrated determination in its wake. "And what's more, I don't tend to get nervous around anyone. Between my military training and the star power, I figure I can handle myself in almost any situation." I looked at Lothian. "But there was something about Victor De Luca that was just... dark. He felt dangerous. Real serial killer vibes." I saw the instant concern in his blue eyes. "I'll be careful. Promise."

"Thank you." His eyes locked onto mine, silently telegraphing his relief that I seemed to understand his concern. "Now, how about we go get some lunch and try to enjoy the rest of this wedding?"

I nodded, realizing I was famished. "Lunch sounds perfect."

Lectures from immortal beings could be exhausting.

The group began to disperse—first, the very smug Apollo, with a quick hug and reminder to call if I needed anything. Getting me to concede he'd been right about any little thing was accomplishment enough in his book.

Lothian opened the sliding glass door for Archie, who insisted he needed to get back to my sisters before Althea's crow ate all of the lunch bacon.

Only Jason lingered, his eyes holding mine in the mirror.

"What?" I asked him.

"You managed to reassure them without saying anything or discussing anything about your feelings. I'm kind of impressed." He looked at my father as he walked out the front door, and in that brief flash, his congenial mask seemed to slip. I caught a glimpse of something hard-edged and penetrating before Jason rearranged his expression and caught my eyes once more. "I just want you to be happy, Astra. You deserve that. You know that, right?"

That he wants me to be happy?

Yeah, I knew that.

That I deserve to be happy?

That was probably a tougher sell at the moment.

"I know, Jason."

He laughed. "You always sound so sincere, but I never know whether to believe you." Even through the icy glass and azure tint of Althea's enchanted Windex, Jason's genial nature radiated warmth. He tilted his head, fussing with the creased collar of that rumpled oxford shirt he always wore, his ever-present smile as effortless as a sunbeam finding its way to flower petals. "I've got to go. We have lunch down here, too, you know."

"Nice. Enjoy your lunch, and say hi to your girlfriend for me."

Jason's gaze flickered to Lothian, something unspoken passing between them. "I'll be sure to do that." He turned to go but paused, glancing at me over one shoulder with a wink and a grin. "I hope you find someone special, too, Astra. And soon."

My muscles twitched with the urge to hurl something heavy at the mirror.

Jason's reflection rippled again, fading into the azure depths of the mirror as though dissolving into hidden cove waters. When it cleared to its chipped hotel mirror clarity once again, I let out a shaky breath.

I was furious at my father—and I knew from everyone's periodic glances at the great god Apollo that this little shindig had been my father's idea. I was grateful to Lothian and Jason for not pressing me on personal issues in front of him. The whole thing had been embarrassing enough as it was.

But a part of me knew my father wasn't entirely wrong—I couldn't keep going like this, building walls against the pain that seeped through, anyway.

The time had come to start facing it, one small step at a time.

# CHAPTER TWELVE

The scarlet vinyl booth squeaked in protest as I slid onto the bench across from Lothian. Mel's All-American Diner surrounded us, seemingly suspended in time somewhere between swing music and sock hops.

Checkered floors stretched out under a sea of chrome and Formica tables. A jukebox crooned in the corner, dispensing tunes for a nickel that hadn't been current since my Aunt Gwennie was a teen. The mouthwatering aroma of diner fare sizzling on the griddle drifted from a kitchen hidden behind swinging doors, teasing my empty stomach with scents of bacon and melted cheese.

I peeked up at Lothian over the top of my menu, noting the way his eyes gleamed in the flickering neon lights. He must have felt my gaze because he glanced up at that exact moment, catching me staring.

A grin quirked his lips.

I frowned into my menu again, flushing under its laminated shield as our waitress, a perky blond named Tammy, stopped by our table. The uniform of a frilly pink skirt and bobby socks radiated vintage Americana charm. "What can I get for you folks today?"

My gaze darted between options like "The Chuckwagon" burger platter, "Blue Plate Special" meatloaf, and "Poodle Skirt Sundae"—a massive hot fudge and nut concoction I imagined could easily serve four.

"I'll have the bacon cheeseburger and fries," Lothian said.

"Make that two." I handed Tammy my menu.

Our perky waitress scooped up the menus. "Comin' right up!"

Lothian leaned forward conspiratorially, linking his fingers on the tabletop as though he were about to share classified intelligence. "Astra, I want to apologize again for that scene earlier. I hope you know I had nothing to do with planning it."

I raised my eyebrow so high it nearly leaped

off my forehead. "Really? You were there, it was our hotel room, and a few of your statements included 'we.' I feel like you had to be at least partially complicit in that nightmare."

"I know you do, but—" Lothian sighed, a rush of breath that conveyed volumes. "Look, it's not easy for me to refuse your father. Given our history and his relationship with what we are. I tried to talk him out of it, but he was determined."

"Ah, I see." I arched an eyebrow. "So I'm like some mafia princess, and you have to cater to my father's every whimsical idea about me out of fear and obligation, or else Daddy dearest will whack you?"

Lothian's mouth opened, a rebuttal visibly teetering on the tip of his tongue. His gaze searched mine across the table, brows drawing together in a familiar expression of concern. "It's not quite like that." Then his mouth twitched. "Okay, it's a little something like that, yes. Your father's requests just come with certain... unspoken pressures I'm having some trouble navigating."

I blinked, surprised by this uncharacteristic candor. His earnest explanation and hangdog expression squeezed a begrudging smile from me.

It wasn't easy for a man like Lothian to claim someone else had control of any aspect of his actions, and I knew the confession wounded his pride just a bit. "Good to know. I'll keep that in mind."

His expression sobered. "Honestly, though, I didn't think dragging Jason into it was appropriate or helpful. I found the whole thing... misguided."

"You don't say." I rested my chin in one hand. "For whatever it's worth, I did pick up on the fact that you and Jason were the only ones in that room who didn't seem to think you had the right to insist on an explanation so you could dig into my reasons and, in turn, give me your two cents. My dad and Archie can go overboard. I appreciated you not piling on."

"Of course. It's not my right to do anything of the sort." Lothian's gaze was intent. "You're one of the most capable people I've ever known. Maybe you are having a difficult time with Jason's passing and your mother's actions—the way I see it, who wouldn't? I have all the faith in the world you'll work through whatever it is that's bothering you. If you do want to talk about anything, you know we're all here for you—and

I'm sure you'll talk to us about it if and when you feel you need to."

"Thanks."

"Meanwhile, I, for one, will cut you some slack when you pull crap like implying I exploit and mistreat women. I'm assuming it's some kind of side effect from grappling with your feelings." He shot me a wink. "Not gonna happen twice, I'm sure."

I dropped my hand to the table, mildly embarrassed by the sincerity in his tone. "Yeah, I'm sorry about that. Honestly, as soon as the words left my mouth, I regretted saying them." Well, not exactly, then. But I did have second thoughts. "I think my mouth just ran away with me."

"I knew that."

Watching Lothian, I remembered a conversation I had with my sisters while we were getting ready for last night's rehearsal dinner.

My sisters crowded beside me in front of the vanity, giggling over memories and inside jokes as they helped zip up my dress and applied their own finishing touches of makeup. Amid swipes of rouge and mascara wands, we talked about men and male stereotypes in relationships.

Althea said the kind of guy every girl should stay away from was the "fixer"—the one who thought he could solve all your troubles or make up for what you lacked. Because, she said, that was usually the type who needed a woman to "fix" to feel like he had a purpose. She then wondered if Lothian was a fixer because of his werewolf nature. Wolves are famous for their strong sense of loyalty and protective instincts toward those they have a connection to.

Sitting there at the diner, I realized that description sounded less like Lothian and more like my father. A godly golden boy convinced of his own infallibility when it came to the human psyche—or, let's face it, anything else he deemed within his realm of expertise. The modern version of the god Apollo even presented himself as a psychologist.

It also sounded like Athena, the goddess who clearly saw herself as some sort of one-woman justice league ready to swoop in and save any mortal she deemed in need of rescue. Without asking, she made me her unwilling pawn and conscripted me into service with warnings hissed in my ear by her know-it-all owl, all because she assumed I would drift without purpose or direction for want of orders to follow.

And claimed it was all a birthday gift, I thought wryly.

"Penny for your thoughts?"

I glanced up from fidgeting with a paper napkin on the table to find those exaggeratedly sapphire blue eyes watching me expectantly, awaiting a response.

He really was stunning.

Lothian's eyes reminded me of the gleaming lapis lazuli stones I collected as a little girl or the vibrant blue shades attainable only with high-quality artist pigments—cobalt, cerulean, ultramarine. Their brilliance often took me by surprise, rendered more startling in contrast with his tousled blond hair and chiseled jawline.

"I was just thinking that while I busted out of my mother's orbit thanks to her untimely death, there are other circles of control I've still got to deal with." I felt heat rise in my cheeks as I fidgeted the napkin right onto the floor, keenly afraid my admiration of Lothian's handsome features and striking eyes were plain to see. "And it occurs to me that some 'heavenly' know-it-alls with millennia of life experience still can't wrap their heads around the idea of free choice," I told him.

With care, Lothian leaned forward and

retrieved the fallen napkin, eyes dancing. "Here, allow me." His fingers brushed mine as he placed the napkin back in my hands, lingering perhaps a beat longer than necessary before withdrawing slowly to rest on the tabletop. "Control and purpose are difficult constructs for immortals to grasp. Eternity is a long time, and they've been playing the same roles for ages. Mortals, though... I believe our lives are meant to be lived and savored, not controlled or directed for the sake of some divine agenda."

"Yet here I am, daughter of one of them and chosen by another one, all these powers dropped in my lap to use on demand. Even if I wanted to walk away from it all, how exactly do I do that?" I smoothed the napkin out on the table. "Sometimes I think maybe it would've been easier if I was just...normal."

Lothian nodded slowly, eyes never leaving mine. "I can understand that. Sometimes this life seems glamorous to others, but it comes with challenges they can't grasp." He sighed. "For us, losing mortal connections and loved ones over time is the most difficult. Seeing history repeat, mistakes of the past forgotten...it can be disheartening."

"Do you ever wish you were normal?"

"What's normal?" he asked with a smile. "Sometimes, I suppose I do. But this is the hand I chose to play." Lothian shrugged. "There are benefits to it as well. And unlike you, I didn't have powers or a destiny thrust upon me—I chose this path, for better or worse. For what it's worth, I think you've done incredibly well, considering many of the things in your life were things you did not choose."

Until he said that, I don't think I truly realized that was the case.

But he was right.

For much of my life, I just accepted.

But I hadn't chosen it.

I cleared my throat. "Thank you, Lothian. I appreciate that."

Maybe Lothian and I had gotten off on the wrong foot, I thought. Or maybe I'd misjudged him. Behind the flashy suits and flirty jokes, perhaps there were hidden depths I never anticipated.

Lothian's gaze darted up as Tammy arrived with our food. She slid two plates piled high with cheeseburgers and fries onto the table, practically beaming. "Enjoy, you two! Just give me a holler if you need anything else."

*  *  *

As Tammy walked away, Lothian's eyes narrowed. He leaned in close, voice dropping to a whisper. "Don't move."

I froze, my hand hovering above a ketchup bottle. "Why? What's wrong?"

"Don't look now, but two booths behind you, against the wall—isn't that Simon Kincaid? And is he sitting with Beatrice?"

I started to turn my head, but Lothian caught my chin, stopping me. "I know you said don't look, but how am I supposed to answer you if I can't move and I can't look?" I asked, my eyebrow raised. Lothian released my chin, and I turned my head slightly.

"That is Simon, right? The guy you saw handing Albert pills?"

I swallowed hard, met Lothian's questioning gaze, and nodded once, confirming that Simon Kincaid sat two booths away with Beatrice, plotting who knew what.

His arm brushed mine as he leaned to peer at his plate, using the pretense of examining his food to whisper at me once more. "I'll keep an eye on them. Can you overhear their conversation?"

I subtly tilted my head to catch snippets of their discussion.

Beatrice's shrill voice rang out. "Can you believe Uncle Albert betrayed me like that? Leaving the station to that idiot DJ instead of me, his own flesh and blood?"

"He didn't betray you, Bea. I don't know why you're always so harsh with him." Simon's tone was soothing. "You know Albert cared for you like his own daughter. But you have no experience running a radio station. He wanted to ensure its future, and the family's future."

"By giving it to Victor? Please. That man's a certifiable nutjob." Beatrice snorted. "Uncle Albert lost his mind. And now I've lost my inheritance!"

"You don't know what you inherited and what you didn't. My dear, Albert was just being practical in giving the station to Victor. And you were never really cut out for that line of work. You had no education in it, no passion for it. Victor, at least, understands the business. Don't be cross with your uncle. I know my poor Albert loved you."

My poor Albert? There was tenderness in Simon's words, an intimate affection, that gave me pause. As if...he and Albert...

Realization dawned.

Albert's secrecy, his being "single" with no children all his life. The care and affection in Simon's tone.

Albert and Simon were involved.

I glanced behind me.

Simon reached across the table, grasping Beatrice's hands. "I know losing Albert has been difficult for you. For both of us. But you have to accept this is what he wanted. What he thought was best to honor his memory and continue the work he cared so much about."

"Oh, my god, you are just so exhausting." Beatrice sniffled in a manner reminiscent of a telenovela actress, dabbing at her dry eyes with a handkerchief for effect. "Why are you always defending him?" She pulled her hands back and crossed her arms in a huff. "You and Uncle Albert were always ganging up against me. Now Victor gets the station, and you get the store. What do I get? I get nothing."

I frowned.

Albert owned Simon's store?

"Beatrice, stop." Simon's tone was firm. "You know that's not true. This isn't about possessions. We both lost someone irreplaceable. I'm trying to help you find closure and move forward like Albert would've wanted."

Beatrice glared at Simon but said nothing.

Wow.

Cousin Beatrice was a real piece of work.

She and my mother would have gotten along smashingly.

Beatrice pushed away from the table and stood abruptly, nearly upending her milkshake. "I've lost my appetite. Betrayal does that. Don't follow me, Simon." She turned on her heel, lips pressed in a firm line, and strode toward the exit without a backward glance.

Simon sighed, dropping his head into his hands as Beatrice disappeared through the double doors. His slumped shoulders radiated weariness, and the deep lines bracketing his eyes spoke of many tears shed in private over his loss. His battle to reason with the tempestuous Beatrice in her current state of distress seemed to take the last ounces of energy from him.

Beatrice's sudden departure and cold demeanor reminded me of a spoiled child denied a coveted toy… the type who would break what she couldn't have rather than see another gain joy from it.

* * *

I SLID out of the booth before Lothian could stop me. He called my name in a hissed whisper, but I ignored him.

Simon looked up as I slid into the booth across from him, surprise etched into the lines of his face. "I'm sorry. Do I know you?"

"We haven't officially met. I'm Astra Arden, Emma Sullivan's maid of honor." I met his questioning gaze evenly, holding out my hand to shake. "And I believe you were Albert Sullivan's significant other."

Simon's eyes widened, and he refused to shake my hand. He glanced around the diner anxiously before leaning forward. "I don't know what would give you that idea, but I assure you—"

"Don't bother denying it," I said gently. "I overheard your conversation. I don't know anyone who heard you speak about him could miss the love you clearly had for Albert." I kept my voice low and even. "You and Albert were romantically involved, weren't you?" I smiled, hoping to reassure him of my discretion and good intentions.

Simon averted his gaze, cheeks flushing. At that moment, I realized how heavily the secret of his relationship with Albert must've weighed upon him, and I wondered why they were forced to hide. "Look, Albert wasn't...we were just close friends. Business partners. I don't know why you would assume—"

"Please don't insult my intelligence by denying what's obvious." I tilted my head, noting the conflict in his eyes. "The truth, Mr. Kincaid. I mean you no harm."

Well, unless you poisoned Albert with that pill you handed him.

But for now, it's the truth.

Simon studied me for a long moment before nodding, tension easing from his shoulders. "Yes, all right? Albert and I were...together. For seven wonderful years." His eyes misted over. "We would have had seven more if his appetites hadn't gotten the better of him." His eyes grew wistful, a sad expression on his face. "He's hidden who he is from his family for his entire life, Ms. Arden. Please don't betray his wishes by outing him now. I didn't agree with it, but I loved him enough to respect him."

"I see." I leaned forward, keeping my tone gentle. "Did Beatrice know about your relationship? That you and Albert were a couple?"

Simon's eyes narrowed. "Why would you ask me that?"

I debated how much to reveal. Simon Kincaid was obviously a suspect—partners killing their partners was a tale as old as time. But I felt (even without reading him) that this was a man loved and lost. His devotion to Albert remained.

"Mr. Kincaid, I met Emma when we both worked at the Forkbridge Police Department together, and Albert's death seems a little... odd to me." The color drained from his face. "I'm trying to get a handle on the truth of Albert's life, get an idea as to whether anyone would have wanted to do him harm. Everyone seems to be writing his death off as the fat man who ate too much, but I'm not so sure it's that simple."

"No." Simon's eyes were wide. "Beatrice didn't know about us. Albert swore me to secrecy, and she believed we were friends. He wasn't ready to come out to his family, afraid of how they might react." He grasped at the table edge as if needing support. "Are you saying you think Albert was... murdered?"

"I don't know. Like I said, I'm just looking into things."

Simon sucked in a sharp breath, looking as if the floor had dropped out from under him.

Albert's death, the sudden loss of the man he loved in secret, and now the possibility that death had not been an accident but part of someone's sinister scheme? Beneath the shock and anguish, a flicker of anger sparked to life in his eyes. "What can I help you with?" he asked.

That didn't sound like a man who murdered someone.

Then again, it could be a man who wanted to keep his friends close and his enemies even closer.

# CHAPTER THIRTEEN

*W*e left the diner to speak somewhere more private, settling at one of the weathered picnic tables tucked into the shade at a local park, a temporary reprieve from the stifling early afternoon heat.

Menacing storm clouds gathered on the horizon, and I knew the blue Florida sky would soon be gray and threatening a downpour. They rolled toward us, darkness chasing away the cheerful blue, the clouds matching the turmoil of emotions that seemed to dance across Simon's face.

When he finally spoke, his voice was scarcely a whisper. "Albert was a good man. He deserved so much more than this life has given him." A wistful smile lifted the corners of his mouth. "When I was with him, all the darkness and difficulties in life would just fade away. He makes me believe I can be more than the sum of my sins."

Albert Sullivan?

The morbidly obese, morally questionable Albert Sullivan that fought his own brother to claim the family fortune, then cut that brother out of it altogether just so he could have all the silver spoons and gravy boats for himself? The Albert Sullivan whose list of sins, recklessness, and greed was probably longer than his grocery bills?

That Albert Sullivan?

"I'm sure he'll get what he deserves in the next life," I said with all the sincerity of a Florida timeshare salesman.

Simon's gaze met mine, eyes glistening. "Do you really think so?"

Before I could answer, Lothian asked how Simon and Albert had met, curious about the details of their relationship and why, in this day and age, they felt it had to remain hidden.

"I didn't. I would have proclaimed our love from the rooftops." Simon smiled, leaning forward, his elbows on the picnic table. "You know, I was just thinking about when Albert and I first met. Pride parade, must've been 2008? He complimented my feather boas. I wasn't sure about him, really, but still… there was something about him."

Lothian raised an eyebrow. "You've been together that long?"

"Well, not officially 'together' at first. But we just clicked and started hanging out all the time. Going out to gourmet dinners, seeing shows." Simon's gaze grew distant, a soft sadness drawing his expression downward. "When I met him, Albert was off by himself, looking adrift in the crowd. Like he wanted to belong, wanted to be a part of it all but just didn't know how, you know? When we met, though, his whole face lit up."

I could picture a younger, more carefree version of Simon in the midst of a Pride celebration. "What won you over about him?"

Simon chuckled. "His knowledge of old radio mysteries and '50s rock and roll. Sci-fi B-movies from back in the day. You name it. Honestly, we never… would never run out of things to talk about."

"When did you become more than just friends?" Lothian asked.

"We moved in together about four years ago,

though we've... we'd been dating for seven. To most folks, we probably still seem like just amiable business partners and roommates." Simon's smile faded into something fonder and a touch wistful. "They don't get to see the side of Albert I do. The little kindnesses and quirks. The way he focuses and taps his foot to songs stuck in his head."

"You sound like you really loved him," I observed.

"What can I say?" Simon's tearful smile returned in full force. "To me, that man's always gonna be the Elvis to my Brenda Lee, the Dean Martin to my Jerry Lewis. We've had these years together, ups and downs, but I wouldn't trade a single day. Not one."

"Why the secrecy about the relationship?" Lothian asked.

"That wasn't me. That was all him. Albert's father used to yell at him for being a 'sissy' when he was a boy," Simon explained, sadness etched into the lines of his face. "He just assumed his family would never accept him for who he was. I didn't agree with staying closeted, and I thought Albert was paranoid, but I loved him enough to respect his wishes."

Lothian asked if Simon had been staying in

Albert's hotel room. Simon shook his head. "No, I have my own room. But Albert gave me a key so I could check on him, unpack for him..." His voice trailed off for a second as if he had gotten lost in the memory. A second later, his eyes refocused, and he continued. "After I heard the news he'd passed, I went to gather his belongings and contacted his assistant to handle the arrangements."

Lothian and I looked at each other.

One mystery solved.

The sorrow in Simon's tone rang true, but there were still too many loose ends and unknowns to cross him off the suspect list entirely. Though his account of tidying up the hotel room seemed plausible, he did remove items in a manner that could have constituted removing evidence. We needed more information so we could decide whether his narrative added up or if Albert's clandestine paramour might have had grounds to want him out of the picture.

I leaned forward, catching Simon's gaze. "Simon, was Albert having any health problems lately? Or was he allergic to anything we should be aware of?"

Simon nodded. "Albert was diagnosed with COPD last year. The doctors wanted him on steroids and inhalers, but you know how stubborn he could be." He sighed. "I gave him homeopathic remedies from my shop—Bryonia, Ginger, Peppermint—to help with the coughing and make breathing easier. But between you and me, I don't think they helped near as much as the real medicines might've."

Peppermint could smell like cough medicine. Under the table, I quickly texted the three remedies to Althea and then looked up. "And the allergies? Was he allergic to anything in particular?"

"Tree nuts. Pecans and walnuts especially. He carried an EpiPen in case of emergency." Simon grimaced. "Peanut butter, too, but walnuts were the worst. Why do you ask?"

"I just want to be sure the authorities have all the information in case any of that's relevant to what happened last night. Since your relationship was a secret, I assume no one's come to talk to you?" I tilted my head, noting the anguish etched into Simon's face.

He shook his head. "You really don't think his death was an accident?"

I leaned back, watching him closely.

I couldn't rule out the possibility he might've had reason to want Albert gone. And since he could be the murderer, I couldn't share what I thought with him. "I don't know. I'm just looking into some things that seem off."

"Off? What seems off?"

"I don't want to share details until I know something for sure one way or the other. It could just be speculation on my part. But if you have any information that you think would help me, please let me know. And again," I said, leaning forward to touch his hand, "I'm so sorry for your loss."

Simon slumped in his seat, the grief plain on his face. Beneath the anguish, a flicker of anger sparked to life in Simon's eyes. "I will let you know if I think of anything. Anything. I want whoever did this to pay for taking him from me."

\* \* \*

As SIMON HEADED off across the park toward his car, a familiar Jeep pulled into the lot behind him.

"They're here," I told Lothian.

"Good timing."

Ami emerged from behind the steering wheel, sunglasses parked on top of her head and an exasperated look on her face. Wyatt climbed out on the passenger side and leaned back to assist

Althea and Ayla in clamoring from the rear seat, the latter hurriedly finishing a call as they approached. Cerberus, the hell hound disguised as a bulldog, waddled along after them.

Althea waved and then plopped onto the picnic table bench. "Well, that was enlightening—and I mean that sarcastically. We didn't find out a lot, but we did discover one thing. I know you said Albert was single, but I don't think he was. I think he was in a relationship and—"

"Hold up, let me guess," I said. "You found out Albert lived with a man, and you think that man was Simon Kincaid."

Ami stared at me. "How did you know?"

I nodded in the direction Simon had gone. "That's Simon Kincaid. We spoke with him after running into him at Mel's Diner."

Ami's mouth fell open. "You're kidding."

I shook my head. "Nope. Simon gave us the whole story. Well, his version, anyway. He and Albert were together seven years, and they lived together for the last four."

"Astra—what did you see when you touched his hand?" Lothian asked.

"Honestly, just a lot of lovey-dovey stuff. Nothing important. His grief is legitimate. It's taken over his mind."

Ami threw her hands up in exasperation. "Great. So that whole trip to Orlando to search Albert's condo was pretty much pointless, then."

"Not entirely," Ayla said. "We know Albert didn't race back there after he died. I mean, he could have." She turned to me. "No ghosts in the condo."

"No, that's true. We know that now." Ami frowned. "And we did check out Simon's shop, too. The employees there said Simon and Albert hardly ever fought and were really good friends. No money problems, no drama. They said Simon's a great boss."

"Yeah, they were really 'good friends,'" Althea repeated, her voice dripping with wry amusement. My sister's fingers curled and twisted into air quotes framing the words.

"Oh, stop it," Ayla told her.

"It's good that we know, actually. Maybe he is telling the truth." I relayed the details of our conversation with Simon, including Albert's COPD diagnosis and severe nut allergy. "Simon seemed genuinely devastated by Albert's loss. But until we rule out foul play, he's still a suspect."

Ami settled onto the bench beside me. "Well, isn't this wedding weekend shaping up to be a real blast." She peered up at the threatening sky.

"And now it looks like it's about to pour. Could this day get any better?"

"Oh, please. This is Florida. It always pours in the afternoon," Althea said.

"Not this early. If it's starting this early, it's going to be a long one."

As if on cue, thunder rumbled in the distance. The storm clouds seemed closer now, nearly blotting out the sun as they continued their ominous advance.

Wyatt glanced at the steadily darkening sky with all the worry and woe of an amateur meteorologist predicting the storm of the century. "We should head back before this storm hits, or Emma will have our heads on pikes for missing the wedding rehearsal tonight."

Ami looked at him. "Head back where? The hotel?"

"Let's go to Arden House," Althea said.

Cerberus barked.

Lothian was staring at Wyatt with utter bafflement. "Okay, let me get this straight. Yesterday was the rehearsal dinner, implying an actual rehearsal took place at some point, even though we didn't rehearse anything. Yet tonight is also deemed a 'rehearsal'?" He scratched his head, eyebrows furrowed. "Why on earth didn't we just rehearse yesterday at the literal wedding rehearsal dinner?"

Wyatt waved his hand dismissively. "You know how Emma is. She wanted a big rehearsal dinner with more than just the wedding party to kick off the weekend, and so that was last night. Tonight is just for the wedding party and the parents—and everyone there knows who we all are. We'll do a quick run-through, but prepare yourself—she'll probably keep tweaking and rehearsing until every last detail is perfect, and we're all teetering on the brink of madness." His eyes took on a haunted look as his imagination ran wild, dreaming up the worst-case dress rehearsal at Emma's mercilessly controlling hands. He looked at me. "Just a friendly warning. Your father will be there, by the way."

"Fantastic," I said. "Just what I need."

"You'll be okay," Lothian said. His exaggeratedly steadfast eyes reflected confidence so implausible it bordered on farcical, as though a few words alone could chase away my father's eons of entitlement.

"How can you sit there spouting such nonsense with a straight face?"

He responded with a wolfish grin, his eyes gleaming as they met mine in a conspiratorial wink. "Fine. I'll keep further pep talks and platitudes to myself. But when adversity arises, and confidence runs thin, just remember: you are Astra. Impossibilities and adversity cower in your wake."

Ami's mouth fell open in astonishment, her eyes wide as she blinked at Lothian.

"What?" Lothian asked innocently.

"If she doesn't date you, I will."

"No, you won't," Wyatt said easily.

My sister made a reeling-in motion with her hands as if to physically pull Wyatt back from his possessive declarations. "Just pump the brakes a bit there, okay?" She expelled a heavy sigh, and her shoulders slumped. "Okay, focus. The good news is we just need to survive one more night of this pink, ruffled tomfoolery. We can handle that. I hope."

"Two nights," Ayla corrected.

"Well, right. Two. Tomorrow's the actual wedding." She stood, brushing dirt from her jeans. "It's not even three in the afternoon, and I already need a drink."

We started walking to the Jeep as the wind picked up around us, hot and heavy as the breath of a dragon's roar heralding an impending apocalypse. This wedding weekend was shaping up to be a regular Pandora's box of complications, drama, and impending doom.

And the storms, both literal and metaphorical, were letting loose.

\* \* \*

THE RAINDROPS PATTERED an erratic rhythm on the metal roof above as we hurried inside Arden House. As soon as the front door thudded closed behind us, Aunt Gwennie's voice rang out from the open doorway off the kitchen leading into the shop. "Astra, you have a visitor!"

Ami glanced at me, brow furrowed. "Are you expecting someone?"

I shook my head.

Lothian and Wyatt followed me through the back door of the house, across the breezeway, and into Spellbound Emporium, the new name of the shop since my mother had passed. The aromatic scent of lavender, sage, and frankincense enveloped us, a familiar and soothing blend of herbs and spices.

Aunt Gwennie stood behind the checkout counter, watching the back door expectantly through wire-rimmed spectacles. Her eyes lit up as we entered, a welcoming smile chasing away whatever worries had creased her brow.

"Hey, Aunt Gwennie. Who's here?"

Archie peered at us from his customary spot on the counter—a wooden platform with arched upright branches (and a bowl of bacon pieces set in the corner). His mottled brown and gray feathers were fluffed as his keen golden eyes followed our unexpected guest with a predatory glare, both curious and calculating.

Beatrice stepped out from the center aisle and leaned against the counter, twirling a lock of hair around one finger. Her eyes roamed the shelves crammed full of crystals, candles, incense, and other new-age knickknacks. There was nothing in her expression, interest, or dress that indicated she would have frequented an establishment like ours under normal circumstances.

"Beatrice?" My tone and expression remained neutral but guarded.

She glanced over at me with a sly smile. "Well, well. I heard rumors the maid of honor and bridesmaids owned some kind of witchcraft shop, but I had to see for myself."

Ami, who'd entered behind Lothian and Wyatt, bristled at the designation. "It's not a witchcraft shop. We sell new-age goods and do readings for all types of people."

Beatrice eyed Ami with exaggerated skepticism. "Right. My mistake." Her gaze slid back to me. "When I saw you sneaking away from the hotel with tall, blond, and handsome over there, I asked around. Hope I'm not interrupting anything juicy between you two, by the way." She waggled her eyebrows suggestively.

I ignored her implication. "What can we help you with, Beatrice?"

She leaned so far onto the counter I worried the glass on the top would break. "Honestly? I'm bored with this dreary wedding stuff. Thought maybe you ladies might liven up the afternoon with some kind of spooky séance or Ouija board session. Maybe a love potion or two?" She shot a coy look at Lothian, who seemed unmoved by her flirtations. "I probably don't need one for you, though. And I bet you're an animal in bed." Beatrice paused. "Are you?"

Well, if that wasn't a double entendre, then I don't know what is.

"We don't do any of those things here. No séances, no Ouija boards," Ami said evenly. "And love potions are unethical."

"Pity." Beatrice took in the scene with a single

sweep of her gaze, lips pursing. "So what is it you do here, exactly, then? Read tea leaves and tarot cards and crystal balls? I just don't see how any of that nonsense is a whit less make-believe than a Ouija board or a love potion."

Ami's eyes flashed. "We offer spiritual and intuitive guidance for those seeking it, and we sell products to help people find their peace and their center. If you're looking to be entertained, I suggest trying elsewhere."

Beatrice waved a ring-laden hand as if brushing away a bothersome fly. "There's no need to get snippy. I was merely asking about your supposed talents. My mistake for thinking this shop might actually be interesting." She started for the exit. "This wedding can't end soon enough. How Emma tolerates this creepy, boring town is beyond me!"

The door slammed behind Beatrice with a bang, her disparaging comments lingering like the cloying scent of her perfume.

"She is really, really unpleasant," Ami said.

Archie ruffled his feathers with enough vexation and pique to start his own personal tornado, annoyance evident in every clipped syllable. "If her ladyship wanted cheap entertainment and absurdity, she should have just gone to the nearest zoo."

I turned to find both Wyatt and Lothian watching me. Wyatt seemed amused, but Lothian's piercing blue eyes held a question I wasn't certain how to answer. "Yeah, I don't know what to make of her little animal crack, either."

"It certainly seemed like she was trying to imply something."

"Well, goodness, dear, I think she was quite forthright with regards to what she wanted from you," Aunt Gwennie told Lothian. A flush colored the werewolf's cheeks, a sight I could count on one hand the number of times I'd witnessed since I'd known him. "It was far more than implication." She raised her eyebrow. "No wonder you're still single if you missed that, young man."

"Aunt Gwennie, we were referring to her comparing him to an animal. It was as if she knew he was a werewolf," I clarified with an awkward cough. "Not the... um, other thing."

"Oh, goodness me. Yes, right you are, my mistake." Aunt Gwennie smiled in embarrassment. "Since our dear friend is indeed rather hirsute and wolfish in appearance at times, I see what you mean."

"You might have a point," Ami said. "Though I think Aunt Gwennie's right. That line worked on two levels." My sister's expression shifted, doe eyes blinking innocently even as her lips quirked in a smile subtly laced with sarcasm. "Did you miss that?"

Lothian studied Ami, eyes slightly narrowed at her teasing. "No, ma'am," he answered, aiming for a respectful response (but unable to keep a hint of embarrassed growl from his tone).

"Nothing else to say?" Ami prodded, eyes dancing with mirth at his discomfort.

Lothian clenched his jaw. "No, ma'am."

"Very wise," Aunt Gwennie noted.

# CHAPTER FOURTEEN

The checklist danced through my thoughts as I started ticking off items. "All right, here's where we need to start."

"So, you're in charge, I take it?" Althea remarked with an arched eyebrow, her tone drier than a desert.

I glared and continued. "Someone needs to talk to the caterer and find out if there were any tree nuts in any of the quiches or appetizers last night. We also need to find out if Albert's EpiPen was on him when they took him to the hospital—and if so, was it used. And we need to look into Beatrice."

Aunt Gwennie's eyebrows knit together in a

cluster of wrinkles. "Why are you suspicious of Beatrice, dear?"

In response to my aunt's question, Althea let out an unladylike snort. "Oh, come on, Aunt Gwennie. Really? You don't think her sly sociopathic demeanor was reason enough?"

"She came in here specifically trying to start trouble." Archie ruffled his feathers, peering down from his perch. "And she wasn't even subtle about it. In fact, that woman wouldn't know subtle if it swooped down and snatched her ridiculous wig right off her vapid head."

"That was a wig?" Ayla asked, surprised.

"I don't think so." I turned to face Archie, taking in his dour expression. "What's with you? Are you still in a bad mood?"

"Whaddaya mean, 'still'?" Archie cocked his head at me.

Wyatt glanced at the wall clock. "I don't mean to rush anyone, but we've only got until sundown. Emma wanted everyone at Sanguine by nine for the paranormal rehearsal dinner."

Althea grimaced, looking as though she'd rather face down an entire evil coven than make idle chitchat for another evening. "Correct me if I'm wrong, but I was under the impression witchcraft came with certain perks. The recruitment flyer failed to mention having to attend twice as many wedding rehearsal dinners."

"Wyatt's right. Sundown is at 8:13 tonight," Ayla said. She glanced up from scrolling through her phone calendar. "We're cutting it a bit close since we all still have to get ready."

I ignored their quips and observations, my mind spinning through the scant details and speculation thus far. "I get that we're busy, but we need to look into Beatrice's background and social media—see if anything seems off. Dig into her financials. She and Albert had argued recently, and she seemed to think she was owed part of his fortune."

Aunt Gwennie frowned, eyebrows pinching together so tightly they almost touched. "You think she might've..." She paused, dropping her voice to a whisper as if about to utter something unholy. "Killed her own uncle?"

Ayla chuckled. "I don't think you need to whisper. We're all thinking it."

I shrugged. "We may be, but I don't know for sure. Her behavior is clearly erratic, and her grievance with Albert seemed pretty intense."

Archie shook, bobbed his head, and snapped his beak. "The woman is mad as a March hare, there's no question," he said. "But is she vicious or cunning enough to commit murder and stage it as an accident in front of a room full of people?"

"We won't know until we look closer." My eyes swept over their faces, my resolve mirrored in the set of their jaws. "We have a few hours to spare before this circus of a rehearsal dinner kicks off. Let's put them to good use and peel back some layers." I turned to Althea. "Did you get my text earlier about the three homeopathic thingys?"

Althea nodded. "The herbal tea recipe?"

I raised my eyebrow. "Is that what that was?"

"Well, sort of. Ginger, peppermint, and Bryonia can be ingredients in herbal teas, but also used in other ways." Althea tucked a lock of hair behind her ear. "An herbal tea blending ginger, peppermint leaves, and Bryonia root in scalding water could, hypothetically, pacify an irritated stomach. Homemade hard candies infused with ginger and peppermint essences might cool an inflamed throat. And muddling mint, grated ginger, and transparent spirits like vodka or gin could, theoretically, get you a healing cocktail for what ails you—or make you need the other stuff the following morning if you drink too much of it."

"So there's no one answer."

"No. The ingredients would most often be used to make herbal tea, but I can't say for sure that's what they were used for. They have other uses and preparations as well. Does that make sense?"

I nodded. "Yes, that helps clarify things." I sighed, trying to mentally review the clues again. "In my vision, I saw Simon give Albert something in pill form the day he died. But I don't know exactly what it was. Since Simon has a shop that sells supplements and natural remedies and Albert had COPD, it would make sense that he would give Albert something from there to try and help."

"COPD?" Wyatt asked.

"Short for Chronic Obstructive Pulmonary Disease. A nasty inflammatory lung disease that made getting it harder for him to breathe. Simon claims he was giving Albert some herbs to help with it."

"And it makes sense. Any of those things you asked me about could be in a pill or a capsule and would help with COPD. The problem is, without knowing exactly what Simon gave Albert or the dosage, it's hard to determine whether it could have interacted badly with anything else he took or ate." Althea grimaced. "Bryonia, in particular, can have side effects and potentially interact with medications, especially in high doses. But in the proper amounts, it's considered safe."

"So it may be a clue, or it may be nothing." I sighed, frustrated by the tangle of dead ends and possibilities. "I wonder if the hospital found anything unusual?"

Althea glanced at her laptop. "I'll see what I can find out."

Lothian glanced at the old cuckoo clock on the wall, its chains and gears clacking and whirring away the remaining minutes until the rehearsal dinner. "We're running out of time here, Astra. What do you want to do?"

"Is anyone friends with any of the paramedics?" I asked.

"We don't get out much," Ayla said sarcastically. "Seriously, though, I spend all my time in Cassandra with Mel." Mel was her boyfriend.

Lothian grimaced with a sidelong glance at Wyatt. "Let's just say werewolves and medical professionals don't exactly run in the same circles, if you catch my drift."

Wyatt nodded. "Our kind sticks to back-alley clinics run by other supernatural beings, thank you very much."

"Great." I sighed. "Fine, I'll go see the chief."

Ayla tossed her hair over one shoulder, the glint in her eye suggesting she relished the challenge. "I'm going to talk to my father." Her red lips quirked at one corner. "See if he knows anything about where Uncle Albert might be."

I released a heavy sigh, dragging a hand down my face. Never mind that her father happened to be Hades, the gloomy ruler of the Underworld. "Must we?" We already had one god dancing around the periphery of all this, silent as a wraith but always watching. Did we have to make it two?

Ayla ignored me.

Althea reiterated she'd dig into Albert's medical and death records as Ami shuffled her tarot cards with the vigor of a Vegas casino dealer. "I'll do a reading and see if I can get any clues."

"All right, everyone keep me posted on anything you find out," I said. "I'm going to head over to the station now and chat with Chief Harmon, see what I can get out of him about the EMTs and their report. Text me updates, but call me if anything urgent comes up. Hopefully, we can get to the bottom of this before tonight."

I snatched up my keys and marched straight for my trusty Jeep when Lothian oh-so-politely coughed, "Ahem, might I suggest we take my car instead?"

* * *

WHEN LOTHIAN SAID "CAR," he really meant his obscenely extravagant eight-cylinder midnight-black sports car. Its paint job gleamed with a shine so lustrous it could put the moon itself to shame, polished to a mirrored finish that seemed to warp the very fabric of space around it. Get stuck behind the thing at a high noon red light, and you'd swear you were gazing into the blistering heart of a supernova if you dared look its way—right before being permanently blinded.

Nothing whispered "I'm a paragon of maturity and restraint" quite like an engine with more cylinders than a Colt.45 and a detailing job so flawless it could be spotted with a high-powered telescope from Jupiter.

Lothian eased into the driver's seat with a cool calm, tweaking one of the numerous interior mirrors just so. His gaze met mine through the reflective glass over the expanse of the console. "You realize we still don't know for certain Uncle Albert was murdered, right?"

"We have nothing better to do," I said. "Your

pack practically hemorrhaged money to ensure this wedding goes off without a hitch. Any hint of upheaval, any misplaced attempt to intervene, and the meticulously arranged plans you guys orchestrated would come crashing down like a poorly built house of cards. Not even the maid of honor has a real job, and not even a murder derailed this pink train."

Lothian pulled out of the driveway in a purr of well-oiled German engineering, the engine throaty enough to rattle windows four houses away. "Oh, come on. It's not that bad. Maybe a little over the top, but she's happy, right?"

"A little over the top?" I made a circling motion with my index finger. "The ice sculptures? The redecorating of the club to resemble a mountain lodge? Burgundy roses? The chandeliers made from antlers? How about the elaborate sugar sculptures of wolves on top of the wedding cake? The multi-tiered wedding cake, mind you?"

"Okay, I—"

"And let's not forget the helicopter seeding the grounds with imported African orchids all in deep purple so the guests on the veranda out back have something to look at... in the dark?"

"A helicopter seeding orchids?" Lothian

glanced at me in disbelief. "I didn't know about that. Are you joking?"

I shrugged, wishing I was. "I can't make stuff like that up."

Lothian swung the sports car into the station's lot with enviable ease, sliding into a spot close to the doors as if he'd willed it into being vacant upon our arrival.

A wave of nostalgia hit me like a brick as the old Forkbridge Police Department appeared. That weathered brick sentinel felt like it held a lifetime of memories behind its walls. A few years of my life were etched into that building, pulling at heartstrings I didn't realize still existed. A bitter pinch of regret nibbled at the edges of happier times.

Gods, I missed it.

I missed the plunge into the fray, the pounding beat of working a hot case. Missed the buzz of unraveling mysteries under Emma's keen eye, my headstrong partner in crime.

My boots had walked every inch of pavement surrounding that place. As much as I enjoyed my newfound freedom and flexibility, a part of me would always mourn having to walk away from a job I'd really wanted.

The second the ostentatious sports car slid

into park, Lothian eased the key to set that kingly engine purring, keeping the air conditioner pumping for my benefit. I looked at him—he looked ahead, but it seemed as if he somehow sensed I wasn't quite prepared to face the circus awaiting inside my old stomping ground. At least not without a few moments of climate-controlled solitude to steel my nerves.

"How did you know I wanted to sit here a few more minutes?" I asked him point-blank. "Because it's obvious somehow you did. Is the sports car ensorcelled or something?"

Lothian looked decidedly uncomfortable.

Then sheepish.

He rubbed the back of his neck, avoiding my gaze as a hint of color rose in his cheeks.

"Werewolves are... extremely intuitional," he said. "We have innate awarenesses we don't need to be taught. We're naturally social, with instinctual ways of communicating with each other using body language, facial expressions, scent. For those I have a bond with and see as part of my... pack, I know more about their state than I might with other people."

"So you can sense how I'm feeling?" I asked.

He nodded, still not meeting my eyes. "To some degree. I could tell you felt strange emotions looking at the station just now. Nostalgia, longing, a bit of sadness. That you weren't quite ready to go inside. My kind is very attuned to the emotional states and needs of … Anyway. Yes. Some."

I pondered that, intrigued and a little disconcerted by this example of preternatural perceptiveness. On the one hand, it could be useful. On the other, the idea of anyone other than my sisters having that degree of insight into my feelings made me uncomfortable. I valued my privacy.

"That seems like it could be either very helpful or problematic," I said.

Lothian's mouth quirked in a wry smile. "I suppose so."

I studied his profile, noticing again how handsome he was, how self-assured. But beneath that veneer, he seemed to harbor depths I had yet to fully fathom. Once again, I realized there was more to Lothian than met the eye—a complexity within him not readily apparent.

And I found that mystery oddly alluring.

We sat in companionable silence for a few minutes. I found his presence oddly comforting, his ability to intuit my moods disconcerting yet oddly reassuring. The werewolf seemed content to simply sit with me until I felt ready to head inside.

Finally, I sighed and reached for the door handle. "We should head in. Sitting here won't get us any answers."

Lothian nodded. "After you."

# CHAPTER FIFTEEN

We climbed out, the late afternoon sunlight glinting off the car's shiny finish, and crossed the parking lot. My heels clicked an unsteady rhythm on the pavement until, at the front doors, Lothian caught my arm.

I moved to pull away and glanced up to find his brow knit in concern. I tilted my head at him, brows arching in question. "What? What is it?"

He hesitated, seeming to debate his next words with care. "Are you sure you're okay doing this?" Lothian nodded toward the building looming before us, all cold glass and steel. "After what happened between you and Jason's mother..." His blue eyes searched mine, etched with quiet concern. "Have you and your captain even talked since then?"

No.

No, we hadn't.

Lothian's unforeseen flash of sensitivity caught me entirely off guard, like a wayward meteor striking Earth. My throat constricted with the ache of temporarily buried hurt as I struggled to dam up tears I refused to shed. Mustering the most reassuring smile I could, I patted his hand. "I'll be fine."

I could look after myself as always, I thought to myself. My hardened armor of cynicism and pride was still firmly locked in place… despite the odd cracks that might show through from time to time.

Lothian nodded, though a muscle feathered in his cheek. "If you're sure." His hand slipped from my arm, fingers trailing reluctantly along my skin as if clinging to this last moment's contact. "And if you say so. But if you need to leave…"

"You'll be the first to know," I promised.

With a final appraising look, Lothian held open the door.

I entered the too familiar station entryway, assaulted at once by the sounds and smells I knew so well. Phones ringing, printers churning out paperwork, stale coffee, and cleaning products. I closed my eyes as a wave of nostalgia crashed over me.

Taking a deep breath, I opened my eyes once more.

Stepping into the station was like stepping back in time.

The worn tile floors were the same. The antique wooden benches were all just where I remembered them. The same clock still hung behind the front desk, its ceaseless ticking keeping the time to confessions and alibis, pleas and bargains, condemnation, and the rare taste of vindication. Its bronze face presided over all like some aloof deity unaffected by the mortal dramas playing out under the harsh lights of its domain.

Beneath the clock sat a familiar figure—Cassie Blackwood, records clerk and queen of gossip, her steel gray curls bobbing as she worked. At first, Cassie looked up with a smile, round face lighting up like a candle. But as I neared the desk, her expression dimmed by degrees. The candle flame guttered and went out.

"Hey, Cassie."

Cassie peered at me over the rims of her eyeglasses, assessing me in a long, awkward once-over. "Astra, dear, what are you doing here?" she finally inquired, her probing gaze and pursed lips suggesting my presence was undesirable.

"I'd like to speak with Chief Harmon if he's available," I said.

Cassie folded her hands on her desk, regarding me with an amalgam of wariness, judgment, and... concern? Her coral-stained lips pressed into a firm line as she gave an almost imperceptible head wag. "Oh, I'm afraid he's in meetings all afternoon. Perhaps I can help you instead?"

My brow furrowed as I peered over Cassie's shoulder. There, in the flesh with fresh donut crumbs clinging to his shirt, was Chief Harmon himself marching across the far end of the station, gesticulating wildly while deep in debate with Officer Briggs. Poor Briggs had the harried look of a man clinging to the last fraying threads of his patience. "Isn't that him right there?"

"Sorry, Astra, but as I told you already, Chief Harmon is booked solid in meetings all day," Cassie insisted again, avoiding eye contact as she fussed with a teetering stack of files like a nervous squirrel. "I can't tell him anything."

I crossed my arms, looking sternly at Forkbridge's long-suffering police receptionist.

"Of course you can, Cassie. Now, please tell Chief Harmon I'm here to see him. Now."

Cassie shook her head, still refusing to meet my gaze as she clung to the dubious excuse of important meetings like a life preserver. "I apologize again, but that's just not possible. The chief can't be disturbed. Is there anything else I might assist you with today, Ms. Astra?"

"Yes," I told her. "You can tell the chief I'm here to see him."

She refused.

Again.

This verbal tennis match of polite refusal and demand volleyed back and forth for a good five minutes with no end in sight. At this rate, Cassie was liable to develop carpal tunnel from all that file rearranging, and my rear end would go numb from sitting on those hard benches waiting for the chief to emerge at quitting time.

Cassie sighed in defeat, abandoning the pretense of busywork to stare at me. "You don't intend to leave without speaking to him, do you?"

I smiled without a trace of humor. "Not a chance."

Lothian chuckled behind me.

She bristled, her spine stiffening, and met my gaze with a glare that could cut glass. "All right, look. The mayor of Cassandra made me swear I'd keep you away from Chief Harmon. Since she's psychic and all, I'm convinced she'll find out if I don't do it. And I'm not getting in trouble for the likes of you, young lady."

The mayor of Cassandra.

Also known as Lillian Thornton.

Also known as Chief Daniel Harmon's girlfriend.

Also known as my deceased ex-boyfriend's mother.

I opened my mouth, ready to protest this descent into absurdity, when the man himself appeared—Chief Harmon in the flesh, filling the doorway behind the reception area like an irritable bull in search of a china shop. His glower landed square on me as his expression curdled into a scowl.

"Astra. In my office, now." He jerked his head toward the corridor behind him, already turning to stomp off without waiting for a response. "Cassie, fetch Mr. Pennington a coffee to keep him occupied. Extra cream and sugar," the chief barked over his shoulder as an afterthought.

I stifled a sigh, hustling after Harmon as he plowed ahead without slowing, scattering various subordinates and bystanders in his wake.

\* \* \*

THE CHIEF GLANCED over his shoulder just once, impatience carved into every hard line and crease of his permanently scowling face as he led me through a veritable maze of hallways. At last, we arrived outside an unmarked door, which he promptly unlocked with a jangle of keys. He pulled the door open with a flourish, gesturing me inside like a surly doorman. "After you." His gravelly tone held all the warmth and good cheer of an undertaker. "Why are you here?"

"Hello to you, too, sir. Lovely day today. No, I've been doing fine. And how have you been?" I bristled at his tone, annoyed at again being treated as if I didn't belong there. "I have a few questions about Albert Sullivan's death. Specifically, the EMT report from last night."

The heavy door creaked shut behind us with an air of finality. "No."

I bit back the first dozen retorts that sprang to mind unbidden, reminding myself only one of us could afford to act on impulse and whim today. He didn't need anything from me. "Look, I get that Jason's mother is still furious with me—"

Harmon folded his arms, exuding impatience the way other men might cologne. "Look, I'm sorry Cassie was rude to you, but Lil's warned the whole town of Cassandra to stay away from witches. Witches, werewolves, vampires. Just you being here will buy both of us an earful."

"I understand why she might feel that way," I said calmly. "But this has nothing to do with her or the town of Cassandra or Jason. Like I said, I'm here regarding Emma's Uncle Albert."

Chief Harmon sighed, his stance softening by a margin so minuscule it took rigorous squinting to detect. "Look, we've got no cause to suspect foul play here. The medical examiner ruled it cut and dry as an accidental choking. Case closed."

I cleared my throat, adopting a patient tone as if explaining simple mathematics to an obstinate child. "With all due respect, sir, it was quiche. People don't choke on quiche." I kept my tone respectful and my expression neutral through heroic effort. "I know my powers make people uncomfortable. But I want to help ensure Emma and Eddie's wedding isn't disrupted further. You closed the case, and that's fine. Don't reopen it. I just want to see the EMT report. Then I'll go."

Harmon considered me for a long moment. I could sense his internal debate, torn between getting in further trouble with his girlfriend and a desire to do right by Emma.

Finally, he nodded.

"Fine. But this is strictly between us. I don't need the town getting stirred up over baseless speculation. And right now, Astra, all you have is baseless speculation about quiche." He stepped out and returned a few minutes later with a thin folder, handing it to me. "The report corroborates the medical examiner's findings, but see for yourself."

I opened the folder, scanning the neatly typed notes and checkboxes. The paramedics arrived on the scene to find Uncle Albert unresponsive, with no pulse, with an obstructed airway. They had attempted to clear his airway and revive him without success. The report noted small red mushroom pieces (with white flecks) and a larger, irregularly shaped piece that had become lodged, completely blocking his windpipe.

I frowned.

"I thought he choked on quiche. Now it's a mushroom?" I showed him the report.

"Maybe the mushrooms were in the quiche. It's all there in writing from the experts, clear as day. Accidental choking—end of story." His tone brooked no argument to the contrary.

"I read him. He didn't choke. His throat closed up."

"You read him?"

I wiggled my fingers.

Chief Harmon looked surprised and grimaced but didn't argue the point. "Be that as it may, we have no evidence to conclusively prove this was anything but a tragic accident. I cannot officially open an investigation without cause."

"I didn't ask you to." I continued flipping through the folder. "I don't see any note that the paramedics found his EpiPen."

"If it isn't in there, they didn't. But if you really want to check, talk to Emma's father. He picked up Albert's effects from the morgue."

"Gotcha." I handed the folder back. "Thanks for allowing me to review this. I'm going to look into this further unless you have any objections."

The chief sighed, scrubbing a hand down his weathered face until I half expected to see a new layer of stubble sprout in its wake. "I'd really prefer you didn't, but you're not under my command anymore, so you do what you want, Arden." He held up his hands in a gesture of surrender. "As long as it's legal."

"Got it."

What he didn't know wouldn't hurt him.

Harmon offered a fatigued bob of his head, the closest I would get to camaraderie.

"Unofficially..." He locked eyes with me, and for a second, I caught a glimpse of the guy I used to work with. "I trust you to be discreet. And I hope you'll let me know if you find anything conclusive."

I agreed, shook hands with the chief, and left the interrogation room. Lothian was waiting by the reception desk, two paper cups of coffee in hand. At my approach, he offered a small smile.

"No luck?"

I liberated one of the coffees from his grasp. "Not in any official capacity. But just between you and me and the wall, something weird did turn up. It could be a big old nothing. But you'll never guess the last name of one of the EMTs."

Lothian's grin broadened. "Yeah?"

"His last name was De Luca."

# CHAPTER SIXTEEN

*M*y fingers tapped a staccato rhythm on my phone screen as I pulled up the search engine. In a few swift strokes, I typed in "Anthony De Luca, Forkbridge." The top hit made my pulse quicken—Anthony De Luca, age 32, Forkbridge EMT.

I leaned forward, scrolling swiftly through the details of his public profile. Jackpot. There, tucked between information about old baseball trophies and 5K race times, was a nugget about his older brother: Vincent De Luca, 37.

The same Vincent De Luca from the radio station. The same Vincent De Luca dating Connie, Emma's cousin and Albert's... niece by marriage? What were the odds?

Probably not high.

I showed Lothian my findings.

"Brothers, huh?" He started the ignition, the sports car rumbling to life with a throaty growl. "They didn't seem to know each other at the rehearsal dinner. I watched the paramedics closely, and the guy acted like he didn't know anyone there." Lothian's smile vanished quicker than a plate of donuts at a police station. "That was quite the performance by our friends, the De Lucas. Whatever else we know, we know they pretended not to know one another."

"Beatrice's personality may make her a great suspect, but maybe we've been too focused on her because of that." I frowned, gaze drifting toward the station doors as I mulled it over. I stared through the windshield at the hulking edifice of brick and steel as everything Chief Harmon said rattled together what we already knew in my mind. "The report says Uncle Albert choked on mushrooms. But you said there were no mushrooms in that quiche."

"There weren't any mushrooms in any of the quiche. There were three kinds of quiche offered: spinach and feta, tomato and Parmesan, and cheddar," Lothian said as he tapped the steering wheel, brow furrowing. "So either the medical examiner got it wrong—"

"Are you sure?"

"I'm sure. I ate it, and I helped with the menu."

"Really?" I said. "Color me impressed with your apparent expertise in the quiche department."

He gave a modest shrug as the corners of his mouth twitched. "What can I say? It's a gift."

The familiar purr of the sports car engine filled the silence as we idled at the curb, watching people come and go from the Forkbridge Police Department. "Okay, so… what do we think? You think this could be an inheritance thing?"

Lothian's hands flexed on the steering wheel, his eyes narrowing at some unseen point in the distance. I could almost see the gears turning in his mind. "It wouldn't be the first time someone killed for the money. It sounded like Albert changed his will recently to leave De Luca the station. Maybe Victor didn't want to wait for cholesterol to do its job."

"We don't know for sure that it was recent."

"We can ask Simon. I know you don't trust him completely, but it makes sense to ask him this. A lie like that would be easily proven false."

"Obviously not," I pointed out. "Since we're

sitting in a car debating what to do next. We'd just go get the will if it was easily proven false."

"It's a weekend, we don't know the lawyer, and nothing like that will happen fast enough to answer questions before the end of the wedding. It would eventually be proven false, though.

"You just pointed out why any option that contains the word eventually isn't really an option." I looked at the time on my phone. "We have to be at the club for the second dinner in an hour and a half." The clock on the dash ticked down the seconds as if counting our hesitation.

Vincent De Luca's proximity and possible motive were concerning, to say the least. The evidence against him was flimsier than my bank account after military payday, and something about this whole scenario felt hinky. I just couldn't put my finger on how all these puzzle pieces might fit together. Victor's ominous confrontation with me on the pathway didn't seem like the brightest idea for a killer trying to fly under the radar.

Unless… he wasn't done.

I rapped my fingers against the window, thoughts churning. After a moment, I turned to Lothian. "We need to look into Vincent De Luca's background. And let's talk to Connie again."

"Okay." Lothian's eyes gleamed with interest. "What are you thinking?"

"I really want to know how De Luca ended up at this wedding. He doesn't know Emma. He doesn't know Eddie." I ticked the points off on my fingers. "Yet somehow, he found a cousin so he could get dragged to it as a plus one. How long have they been dating? Where did they meet?" I met Lothian's gaze. "I want to know."

He nodded. "Connie's staying at the hotel. Want me to do some digging?"

"She's staying at the hotel with De Luca?"

Lothian shook his head. "No. I overheard her talking to Emma. She just wanted to be close to the action and not have to run back and forth to Orlando. But they're not staying together. At least it didn't sound like it."

Then what was he doing creeping around the garden paths?

"Roger that," I said. "Let's reconvene at the hotel then. You can do some incognito investigating into Victor's background via Connie."

"You got it, Sherlock." He winked.

The moment Lothian slammed the gearshift into reverse, I braced myself. The sports car's engine let out an indignant roar, and we pulled out of the station lot in a cloud of acrid smoke, tires shrieking in protest. The needle on the speedometer trembled and climbed as we hurtled down the road.

"Are you trying to get arrested?" I asked.

"I've never gotten into an accident, and I've never gotten a ticket." He shot me an amused sideways glance. "Are you telling me you don't enjoy speed?"

"In front of a police station? No."

For a couple miles, I kept one eye on the rearview. I half expected to spot the flash of red and blue in the mirror and hear the wail of sirens demanding we pull over this instant. But when no squad car appeared to crash our party, the fading adrenaline buzz convinced me either the Forkbridge Police had bigger fish to fry tonight or they were all too busy hanging out at the local church's annual fish fry, stuffing their faces and guzzling brews to care about minor infractions like reckless driving.

Hard to say.

"You take too many chances," I told him.

"And you don't take enough of them."

I opted not to argue as the car rumbled with untamed power and vigor, mirroring whatever was brewing between us that felt as charged as the air before a storm.

\* \* \*

THE HOTEL ROOM balcony provided a front row seat to the spectacle of the resort's sparkling pools and cabanas under a curtain of golden sunshine. I sidled up to the railing, feeling the warmth of the flagstones radiate through my sandals as the late afternoon sun worked its magic.

Many wedding guests were still enjoying the pool, tanned darker and burned brighter than they were that morning. Those unfortunate souls who'd underestimated the sun's intensity wouldn't realize they'd burned until they went inside, the damage already done.

For a second, I wondered if dear old Dad, the sun god Apollo himself, had made it a point to take his winter vacation in Florida simply because the sun packed more punch. In Florida, showing anything less than the utmost reverence and respect for the sun's savage power could leave you saddled with blisters, headache, a fever, and a case of nausea worse than if you ate discount gas station sushi.

I watched Lothian walking along the edge of the pool toward Connie. She was stretched out on a lounge chair in a scarlet bikini soaking in the remaining rays of the day. The werewolf greeted her, adopting an easy, flirtatious posture I was all too familiar with. Even from this distance, I could see the smile he flashed her could charm a nun.

Connie seemed receptive to his charms, giggling at something he said.

I felt an unexpected prickle of annoyance at the display unfolding below.

Lothian looked entirely too comfortable in just swim trunks, all tanned muscle and careless grace. His arms folded over a bare chest so broad you could land a plane on it as he leaned over her with a cocky sureness. Lothian oozed the casual magnetism of a predator on the prowl and moved with the lethal grace of peril gift-wrapped in one seriously tempting package.

What an epic tool he'd been when we'd first crossed paths, I reflected. And truth be told, he'd carried on being a complete tool—a veritable He-Man of tools, if you will—right up until...well, right up until he decided he could trust me, I supposed.

Hadn't I been a jerk to people in the military at times?

And even more so to people who weren't part of my inner circle?

I heaved a sigh, sagging into the heat-soaked stone railing like it alone was propping me up. As loathe as I was to confess it, maybe Lothian and I were far more kindred spirits than I cared to admit.

The sound of the door opening and closing behind me shook me from my reflections. I turned to find Ami stepping onto the balcony, dressed for the evening's festivities in an emerald green cocktail dress that complemented her eyes.

"There you are! I brought your dress for tonight, but I forgot to bring you the shoes that matched," she told me, gesturing inside. "You can't go in the ones you wore last night. What are you doing out here?" She peered over the railing with the keen curiosity of a scientist observing some fascinating new species in the wild at the scene unfolding below by the pool.

"Nothing. Just watching."

The sounds of frolicking tourists splashing and caterwauling with abandon drifted up to our lofty vantage point, muffled into a cheerful din by a jungle of palms and a riot of bougainvillea blossoms set ablaze in the day's fading golden glow.

"Astra, why are you glowering at Lothian like that?"

"What?" I blinked, realizing I had been staring rather intently at Lothian among the poolside waiters in crisp white shirts. "I'm not glowering. Just... avidly observing. Making sure that flirtation gets us some useful information, that's all."

Ami shot me a look that said she knew precisely what I'd been avidly observing. "Okay. I will pretend I buy your explanation because I don't have time to get into it." She clapped me on the arm with mock sympathy. "Come on. Emma's second rehearsal dinner kicks off in forty-five, and if we're late, she'll serve us for dinner."

With that, my nosy sister ducked back into the hotel room, leaving me once more alone on the balcony with my convoluted thoughts.

Alone again, I gazed down at Lothian chatting with Connie by the pool.

He leaned into her personal space with that roguish grin and a casual hand on her arm. His body language and attentive mannerisms screamed flirtation, and Connie seemed thrilled to be the recipient of his charm offensive. Lothian could pour honeyed words and his natural charisma over anyone who caught his eye —it was his nature.

I knew that.

So why did watching him in his element twist something in my chest? I frowned as another unwanted stab of annoyance caught me by surprise, and I felt a flicker of—what, jealousy?

Absurd.

That's absurd.

Get a grip, I told myself.

Despite my self-lecture, I couldn't quite tear my gaze away from the cozy scene unfolding below. The tangle of feelings Lothian provoked refused to be ignored.

Which was stupid, I thought.

It was not like he was the type of man to settle into quiet domesticity, and I was hardly an ideal candidate for it, either. I was the eldest in a family of witches, the first to forge my path outside everything my mother had carefully built. The only one of my sisters that had ever lived free of my mother's influence. I had a responsibility to help them do that for themselves now that my mother was gone, and they were the masters of their own destiny.

Then again… who better to understand the pull of family and commitment than a werewolf devoted to his pack? Lothian might respect my independence and my devotion to my family. I sighed. Great. But who can build a relationship with two people like that? Or it could be even worse. He could ask for pieces of me I wasn't ready to give.

Not to him.

Not to anyone.

"Astra, did you not hear me calling you?" Ami's voice cut through my turbulent thoughts. I turned to find her standing in the doorway, hands on her hips. "You have to get ready—you only have thirty-five minutes until you need to leave, and you haven't even showered! I have to head back to Arden House to get Althea and Ayla, but I am not leaving until I get you in a shower, at least."

I gave the pools below one last glance.

As if sensing my eyes on him, Lothian looked up. Our gazes locked across the distance, a frisson of connection sparking in the space between us.

For a heartbeat, the rest of the world fell away.

There was only Lothian and the promise of something more in his eyes, something that set my pulse racing for reasons I didn't want to think about.

I turned away from him and went inside.

\* \* \*

I EMERGED from the billowing steam clouds of my shower wrapped in one of the hotel's plush white robes. The hot water had washed away the tension and tangled thoughts of the balcony, if only temporarily, knots in my shoulders finally loosening their hold.

I felt almost normal.

Securing the robe around me, I headed into the adjoining bedroom. The shower might have washed away the surface worries and distractions of the evening, but underneath it all, the questions remained.

I chuckled to myself.

Where Lothian was concerned, almost normal was the closest I could get.

The steam-soaked peace I had found scattered like grains of sand as Lothian strode through my hotel room door. He reeked of coconut suntan lotion and sunshine that seemed to cling to his skin.

My annoyance flared.

He had ten minutes to make himself presentable before we needed to leave for the rehearsal dinner. Ten minutes. I eyed his tousled hair and the open shirt that revealed a glimpse of his chest. It would take nothing short of magic to transform him in time, and it wasn't the type of magic I did.

Lothian's gaze met mine, a question in those eyes. I sighed, grabbing for the patience he always seemed determined to test. "You're late," I told him. "Did you forget we have another rehearsal dinner to get to?"

His lips quirked into that familiar half-smile that never failed to make something inside me twist lately. "I'll be ready with time to spare. Promise."

When Lothian emerged from the bathroom minutes later, adjusting the tie I had been sure wouldn't make it within ten feet of his neck before the dinner started, I wanted to clobber him. Preferably with something that would wipe that smug smile off his face, if only for a moment.

He caught my expression and frowned, brows knitting together in confusion. "Astra?"

"What?"

"Did I do something wrong?" The werewolf fetched his wallet and keys, distractedly checking his reflection in the mirror. But his eyes kept wandering back to me, searching my face as if the answer might be there.

"We're going to be late," was my only response. I grabbed my evening bag from the dresser, striding past him out the door.

"But I thought dinner didn't start for another twenty minutes?" I turned back to see him checking his watch as if I might be mistaken. "Have I misread the schedule?"

I turned to glare at him, irked for reasons I couldn't fully articulate, and he probably wouldn't comprehend even if I tried. "Are we going or not?"

Lothian hesitated, unsure of how to respond.

He started to reach out but seemed to think better of it, fingers clenching around his keys instead. "Have I done something to offend you?" The werewolf's stunning blue eyes searched mine looking genuinely worried I might say yes. "If I did, I'm really sorry."

I stared into those worried eyes and felt that blasted sensation twist inside again.

How did he do this to me?

"Don't worry about it." I turned on my heel. "Come on, we'll be late." I quickened my pace but could sense him following a step behind, still wondering, no doubt, what he had done wrong.

Part of me wanted nothing more than to assure him the offense was mine alone, but that was a confession that would reveal too much.

"Look, whatever I did, just... yell at me in the car, okay?" Lothian pulled his keys from his pocket, unlocking the sleek sports car at the curb with a chirp. "I did get some info. After you yell at me, I'll get you up to speed on the way over. Deal?"

I slid into the passenger seat without looking at him, closing the door a bit too firmly.

Lothian folded himself into the driver's seat, starting the ignition with a throaty roar of the engine. After a few minutes of tense silence, Lothian glanced at me sidelong with a rueful smile. "So are you going to yell at me now, or do I have to wonder what I did all night? I know I told you I was instinctive, but I'm not that instinctive."

I kept my gaze fixed out the windshield at the sun dipping lower on the horizon, a blaze of gold and pink against the darkening sky. My feelings were my own to deal with, not his. I forced a smile, hoping it appeared more genuine than it felt. "It's nothing. Don't worry about it. I thought you were going to tell me what you found out."

Lothian nodded slowly, though the crease

remained between his brows. "Are you sure you're all right?"

"This drive isn't overly long, wolf. You might want to get to it." I waved a hand, feigning nonchalance. The sooner he told me what Connie had revealed, the sooner I could refocus on the case rather than the unwelcome realization of how worried he seemed about my frustration with him and how sexy his concern made his face look.

His worried gaze lingered on my face a moment longer before returning to the road. "If you say so." Lothian tapped his fingers against the steering wheel. "Connie didn't give too much away under that bubbly, flirtatious act—if it was an act. But she did let a few key details slip..."

# CHAPTER SEVENTEEN

The valet's hand gripped the handbrake of Lothian's sleek black bullet of a car as I pushed out of the plush leather seat. I could feel the heat coming off the sun-warmed asphalt of the parking lot, even though it was well into dusk.

"Astra?"

"I'm going in," I said and hurried toward the door. I needed space to breathe, to gain perspective on the snarl of unwanted feelings the werewolf's sandalwood scent and cerulean gaze stirred within me.

"Astra, what's the matter?" Lothian called as I hastily made my way into the club.

I didn't answer.

Inside the dimly lit foyer of Sanguine, I paused to smooth the lines of my dress and collect myself. The familiar scents of the age-old stone Rex had imported mixed with the lemony scent of wood polish, and it grounded me as I strode into the main dining hall. A new and intoxicating mélange of smells took over—rich wine, roast meat, and the buzz of relaxed magic.

"Astra!" Elizabeth, Emma's mother, walked over with baby Hunter cradled safely in her arms. A much older woman hurried behind her like an energetic puppy, eager for any opportunity to take the infant. "Have you seen the baby today? Because if you haven't, you should come get a snuggle or two in."

"Hi, Mrs. Sullivan," I said with a brief smile.

Elizabeth smiled back, though her gaze remained distracted by the baby. "Good evening, my dear. So glad you and Lothian made it on time. Oh, allow me to introduce Emma's Aunt Mildred. I don't think you've met."

The older woman blinked up at me from behind a pair of spectacles that had gone out of fashion decades ago, wispy gray hair escaping a rather haphazard bun. But her eyes gleamed bright with delight at the baby, and she grasped my hand fiercely in both of hers. "You're our

Emma's very best friend, aren't you? Oh, you're as pretty as they said you were!"

Instantly, a flood of visions surged through my mind with dizzying speed.

A little girl with pigtails and skinned knees, sobbing in her mother's embrace. The bittersweet triumph of a high school graduation, caps flung into the air. An ivory wedding gown and the crushing heartbreak of betrayal. The wonder of new life, holding her infant daughter Connie for the first time. Days and sleepless nights of motherhood where she worried that her daughter would never settle down, would always be obsessed with conspiracies...

With an iron force of will, I wrenched my hands from her grasp and staggered back. "How do you do?" I managed.

"Oh, dear, you're the one that can see things with a touch, aren't you?" Aunt Mildred beamed, pumping my hand with surprising vigor before dropping my hands like they'd burned her. "Oh, my goodness me, I did it again!"

"It's all right," I stepped back out of her reach so the floodgates of memories would slam shut. "Don't worry about it."

"So sorry, so sorry! This is all new to me!" she said before turning that megawatt smile on the baby. "I'm just so honored to be let in on the little secret." she said. She looked up and smiled at Rex, who was talking to a group of vampires on the second level. "Well, two secrets, really." Then she looked at me. "Three secrets now, I suppose!"

Elizabeth's expression softened as she gazed down at her grandson. "This little guy has certainly changed quite a bit for everyone, hasn't he?"

"Yes, he has!" Aunt Mildred's face lit up as if it were Christmas morning. She clapped her hands together, peering at the infant. "Aren't you just precious?" Hunter blinked at the effusive woman currently showering him in adoration and promptly stuffed one tiny fist into his mouth, seeming uncertain how else to respond.

A smile tugged at my lips as I watched them.

This rehearsal dinner was limited to paranormals and paranormal-friendly humans in the know about supernatural life in Forkbridge. Some guests, like some of Rex's vampire friends and the pixies, would attend only this dinner. Those who could hide what they were, like my sisters and I, would be around for the full wedding weekend.

"Astra," Lothian said as he stepped beside me.

Before I could react, the baby did. At the sight

of Lothian, Hunter let out an excited squeal that turned every head in the whole club in our direction. His chubby arms waved, tiny hands grasping eagerly for the werewolf.

I blinked in surprise, glancing between the pair.

Lothian's expression softened as he gazed down at the baby, the corners of his eyes crinkling. "Well, hello to you, too, little man." He grasped one tiny hand in his, giving it a gentle shake as if Hunter were an old friend. "My, haven't you grown in the last couple of days!"

Hunter let out a bubbly giggle, pudgy hands grasping at the air as he tried to catch Lothian's hand once more as it pulled away.

"Are you trying to grab my hand? Are you?" Lothian made a series of ridiculous faces, puffing out his cheeks and crossing his eyes, eliciting another gleeful squeal from Hunter.

"I think he missed you," Elizabeth told Lothian.

"Well, I know I missed him."

With tenderness I wouldn't have believed possible, Lothian scooped the infant into the air, nuzzling his nose against Hunter's belly until the baby erupted in a fit of hysterical laughter.

"Oh, Lothian," Elizabeth smiled. "You do always seem to cheer him up."

"I bet I could cheer him up, too. Here, let me try." Mildred hovered nearby, hands twitching with the urge to pluck Hunter from Lothian's arms. "May I? Please? Yes?"

The werewolf relinquished the baby into Mildred's waiting hands with an indulgent smile, and the older woman immediately began making ridiculous faces at Hunter, who squealed in delight at this new game. She drifted with the baby toward an older man, Lothian following.

Elizabeth turned her attention to me, drawing me into a warm hug. "It's so good to see you, Astra. And yes, I know I just saw you yesterday, but I've heard you two have been off chasing information about Thomas's brother. I worried you wouldn't be coming."

"We have been, but we wouldn't miss this." I returned her smile. "Emma would have strung us both up by our fingernails in the pixie swamp if we missed this dinner."

Elizabeth laughed. "I'd love you tell you you're wrong, but you're not wrong. She's still furious with the chief that he didn't show up because of the... well, anyway, I'm glad you're here."

Because of me.

He didn't come because of me.

Her gaze drifted past me to where Lothian stood conversing with a few other dinner guests, Hunter still giggling away in Mildred's arms. "You know, Astra, Lothian's surprisingly good with Hunter. Look at him, watching to make sure Hunter's all right. It's too bad he hasn't found someone to settle down with. I think we all hope that changes soon."

Something in her tone gave me pause, and I turned to study Elizabeth's face. Her polite smile revealed nothing. "Yes, it's too bad."

Emma's mother laughed. "Oh, Astra, don't look at me like that. I'm no witch, but I know without a doubt that man is head over heels for you, plain as day." Elizabeth patted my arm, her meaning now unmistakable. "I should rescue Hunter before Mildred tries to slip him into her purse. We'll talk more after dinner!"

With that, Elizabeth glided off to collect her grandson from his overzealous aunt. I watched them go, mulling over her parting words, and wondered if, where Lothian was concerned, I was the only one who remained oblivious.

\* \* \*

AMI SIGHED, gazing at me with an all-too-knowing look. "You're not oblivious, Astra."

I opened my mouth to protest, but she cut me off with a shake of her head.

"You're stubborn. There's a difference."

My jaw snapped shut with an audible click.

Ami didn't so much as bat an eye. "You see everything you want to see. But when there's something you don't like looking at?" She threw up her hands in mock frustration. "All of a sudden, you're blind as a bat."

"All right, oh wise one, you've made your case. I'm stubborn. Bullheaded. Pig-ignorant." I glowered at her. "Satisfied?"

A cheeky grin was her only reply.

The dining area was arrayed with intimate round tables covered in crisp white linens and adorned with flickering candles. My family was assigned a table near the front, close to where Emma and Eddie sat at the rectangular table elevated on a dais. Waiters (brownies brought in from who knew where) glided silently between the tables, depositing plates of appetizers and filling glasses of wine.

Ami and her date, Wyatt, one of the other werewolves from Eddie's pack, sat to my right. They were holding hands under the table and gazing at one another with all the besotted wonder of new love.

Across from me, my littlest sister Ayla chatted animatedly with her boyfriend Mel, a citizen of Cassandra (who was defying the mayor to be here.). And beside Mel, my sister Althea was deep in conversation with my father, the god Apollo, wearing one of his customary mortal guises.

At the front of the room, Eddie grasped a wine glass and tapped it with his spoon, the clear chime slicing through the chatter. Conversation faded as heads swiveled in unison toward the sound. "Our ties to the supernatural community —here in Forkbridge and throughout Central Florida—mean the world to us. We hope to add our pack's den to the rich paranormal history already here, and we know it's because of friends like you that the preternatural world continues to thrive in Forkbridge."

Emma stepped up beside her groom, slipping an arm around his waist. "Eddie and I know that a bond like the one we now share with all of you is a blessing not afforded to all. Your love and support have guided us to this moment, and we look forward to navigating the adventures to come...together, as always."

Eddie raised his glass in salute. "To friendship,

love, and lifelong partnership. To facing every challenge and seizing every joy...side by side, come what may."

A quiet smattering of applause went up at the couple's heartfelt words.

Against all logic and reason, they had somehow navigated a battlefield of obstacles, setbacks (and poor relationship choices on Emma's part) to find their way into each other's arms, ultimately proving that every now and then, love really could overcome all manner of tomfoolery.

As the applause died down and conversation resumed, Lothian leaned closer to murmur in my ear. "Elizabeth told me that Aunt Mildred is actually Connie's mother. Did she say anything at all about Connie? Or did you read her when she grabbed your hands?"

I smiled, glancing sidelong at him. "I got some images, but nothing specific. Older people can be pretty hard to read. They have a lifetime of memories swimming around in there, and weddings make everyone nostalgic."

"I notice she's not here."

"Nope. The question is did she skip it because she's not in on what we all are, or was she not trusted with the information?" I took a sip of wine and looked around. "I see a few empty chairs. She may have just skipped it."

Lothian's gaze drifted across the ballroom to where Emma stood, her smile glowing as she accepted embraces and well-wishes from various guests. "Nothing she said down at the pool indicated to me that she knew about any paranormal anything," he said. "But I still think it was odd. If she's been dating De Luca for two years, like she said, paranormal talk must be a big part of their relationship, right?"

I let out an unladylike snort. "When did you become a relationship expert?"

Lothian chuckled, a low rumble I felt more than heard.

"Honestly, though, when I met her at the first dinner thing, that's how she explained who De Luca was," I told him, my voice low. "That he was that guy from the Midnight Hour. She seemed surprised that there was a possibility we hadn't heard of him."

"I think we should try and ask Aunt Mildred about Connie and Vincent. I still think it's just odd that she wouldn't say anything about paranormals at all." His eyes crinkled with a knowing smile, and he leaned. "And maybe we'll stop by and invite Vincent and Connie out for a drink later."

Our waiter materialized silently beside us, pale and wan as a specter in his tuxedo. "Sir, madam, will you have the filet mignon or poulet Bresse this evening?" His obsidian gaze darted between us as he proffered a deep bow, gloved hands trembling. "If you'd like a whiff, I can provide that. The filet," he said. A bouquet of juicy beef and truffles escaped as he opened the menu with a crisp snap. "And now, the chicken," he said, closing the menu and opening it again to produce steam scented with garlicky chicken.

"The filet," Lothian told him.

"Okay, that's cool," I said, pointing at the menu. "Where do I get one of those?"

"You don't," the waiter scoffed, pointed nose in the air. "What are you eating, witch?"

I blinked, unused to being looked down upon by a creature scarce tall as my elbow. "Um. The chicken, please. Thank you."

"Right." His cravat seemed to ruffle indignantly as he turned with a sniff, polished boots clicking impatiently on the wood floor.

"I don't think the waiter likes witches," Lothian said.

"Most brownies don't."

My father rested his elbows on the table, steepling his hands and regarding me with a polite smile. It was the one he used when keeping up appearances. "Astra, how goes the investigation into Albert's death? Have you made any progress?"

Though his tone was light, I detected the sharp glint of curiosity in his gaze. And something harder. Impatience, perhaps. I took a deliberate sip of wine to avoid answering.

When I finally met his stare, I kept my expression neutral and my voice bland. "I'm not discussing that with you. In fact, I think I've decided I'm not discussing anything with you." I paused. "Dad."

All conversation at the table stopped, and my sisters watched.

His smile tightened by a fraction. A flicker of annoyance behind his eyes, there and gone. "I was merely inquiring how it was going. Why so hostile?"

"Why so hostile?" I asked. "Really?"

"Astra, I—"

"Because you had no right to drag Jason back from the underworld just so I could 'work through my feelings,'" I said sharply. I resisted the urge to squirm under his scrutiny, though his oddly mild gaze unsettled me for reasons I couldn't quite pinpoint. "That was cruel and manipulative. Because the last time we talked, you told me I shouldn't even be looking into this. Now, suddenly, you're asking me how it's going, like you're supportive? Doesn't work like that. We're done talking about this."

"Of course," he replied, a chill entering his tone. "You're angry with me over that. I'm sorry, Astra. I thought I was helping in my own misguided way. I can see now that was a mistake."

"Whatever." I was in no mood to assuage anyone's discomfort, least of all Apollo's.

Apollo cleared his throat, turning to Althea with a smile that didn't quite reach his eyes. "So, Althea, how goes your study of alchemical manuscripts these days?"

Althea seemed surprised to find herself the sudden recipient of my father's undivided attention but launched into an enthusiastic summary of her latest research. The tension eased as the conversation turned to lighter topics, though things remained slightly stilted between Apollo and me for the duration of the meal.

\* \* \*

AS THE DIN of chatter rose around us once more, servers swarmed in to clear the remains of dessert. The dining area erupted into activity, brownies weaving between tables with practiced efficiency. Amid the flurry, Emma wandered over to us, her steps unhurried as if she had all the time in the world.

"I'm really glad we decided to do this. I just wish Uncle Albert could have been here," she said. "He was so looking forward to finally meeting everyone in person."

Wait.

What?

I blinked. "Your Uncle Albert was supposed to attend tonight?"

Emma nodded. "We'd been easing him into the truth about the supernatural world little by little, saving the big reveal for this weekend. He was excited to meet Eddie's pack at last. Family is family, you know?"

So Albert's comment to Lothian, the one about the pack.

He did know. But...

I stared at Emma in disbelief.

Why would Uncle Albert leave his radio station to someone hell-bent on exposing the paranormal community if he supported them? If he knew they were family now? My confused eyes met Lothian's, and the frown creasing his brow told me he shared my confusion.

Emma's father, Thomas, wandered over as our exchange tapered off. He sighed, resting a hand on her shoulder with a gentle squeeze. "I'm sure your Uncle Albert is here with us in spirit tonight."

Thomas glanced at Ayla, brows raised in question. She gave a faint shake of her head. His expression shuttered for a heartbeat before clearing once more.

"Well, regardless." Thomas offered Emma's shoulder another pat, smile returning, if a shade dimmer. "We only told your uncle bits and pieces about Eddie and the pack. Just enough so tonight's full introduction to our family's paranormal world wouldn't send him into cardiac arrest." A wry chuckle escaped him. "Family is family, for better or worse."

"I don't mean to be rude or anything, but I don't understand." I turned to Thomas with a frown. "How can you be so sure he could be trusted? Didn't he kick you out of your family inheritance?"

"I don't know that I'd put it that way. I was never interested in running a business, and Albert never refused me if I needed cash for something important."

"Uh-huh," I said, sounding more disbelieving than intended.

"Astra, we had our differences at times, but Albert was still family." Thomas shrugged. "My brother could hold a grudge, it's true, but his loyalty to the family always won out in the end."

I cast a sidelong glance at Ami. She caught my eye, brows quirking in silent question. I gave a faint shake of my head, hoping my hunch was mistaken. If Thomas's account of his brother was accurate rather than a fanciful delusion, our entire approach had been wrong.

Dead wrong.

If Uncle Albert had been so supportive and excited to meet Eddie's pack, why choose Vincent De Luca, a known paranormal conspiracy theorist working to expose that paranormal, as heir to his radio station?

And why cut Beatrice out of her supposed inheritance so soon before finally revealing the truth to Uncle Albert about Emma's new extended "family"?

# CHAPTER EIGHTEEN

*A* mournful violin rose above the chatter, drawing curious glances. Shadows stirred at the far end of the club's dance floor, and the dais emerged into golden light.

A tall, lanky man carrying a violin stepped forward, his raven hair stark against preternaturally pale skin. He offered a stiff bow, a smiling expression that seemed to be carved from marble. "Good evening. We are the Children of the Night. We hope our music pleases you." His voice had the sonorous quality of an opera singer with an accent as thick as the snow in a Russian winter.

"They've been playing for over two centuries," Rex said proudly. "We're lucky we got them."

The violinist turned, coattails flaring dramatically like raven's wings. At a silent cue, the others lifted their instruments—two violins, a cello, and double bass. Bows danced across strings with preternatural grace playing something I didn't recognize, an odd combination of ethereal and snappy.

A pixie couple with shocks of emerald hair instantly dove onto the dance floor, and the hypnotic beat of the music quickened. Other pixies quickly joined him, and soon Sanguine's wood dance floor was awash in whirling and frenzied splashes of color. The pixies' joyous laughter pealed high and bright, an ancient celebration that would dazzle jaded mortal senses if they ever saw it.

Of course, most never would.

I felt a tap on my shoulder and turned to find Lothian behind me, hand extended in invitation. "May I have this dance?" His eyes gleamed with warmth and... something more. A tenderness that caught me off guard.

Before I could respond, my father materialized at Lothian's side, and his focus shifted to me without any preamble. "Astra, would you do me the honor?" Apollo asked with a polite smile.

I blinked, slightly annoyed by the interruption. "Now?"

He gave a brisk nod. "If you please."

I shot an uncertain look at Lothian, but he merely shrugged, features giving away nothing of his thoughts.

Wimp.

I wanted my father to buzz off, but I didn't have the patience to get into it with him again. Frowning, I pushed to my feet and came around the table. "Sorry to you both, but I was about to ask Thomas for a dance. I have a few more questions about Albert. You know how it is. Maybe later?" Without waiting for any response, I made a beeline for Emma's dad, weaving away from the two men through the guests clustered at tables nearby.

Thomas looked up as I approached, brows lifting in polite surprise as I asked him to dance while Hunter bounced up and down on his lap and giggled.

He opened his mouth with a regretful expression, no doubt about to offer some courteous refusal, but his wife quickly intervened. "Of course she can have a dance, Thomas!" Elizabeth plucked the baby from her husband's lap and shooed him off toward the dance floor with an impish smile. "Go on, darling. I'll look after Hunter. Don't you worry."

Thomas gave his wife a bemused glance but rose without further protest. He shook out his shoulders and offered me his arm, the big man as courtly as a regency romantic. "Shall we, Astra?"

Thomas smiled down at me as we moved across the dance floor, steps unhurried. "You look lovely tonight, Astra. Though I must confess, your invitation to dance caught me off guard. I thought you'd want to spend dance floor time with Lothian."

"Well, I should probably confess I have an ulterior motive."

His brows rose, surprise shifting to wariness. The change was subtle, a flicker behind genial humor, but I marked it all the same. "Oh?"

"I wanted to ask you about your brother. The picture I have so far... is not entirely clear."

Thomas sighed, the lines around his eyes deepening. "I see. Go on, then."

"You said Albert could hold a grudge but was always loyal to family. Do you really think he would've accepted all the paranormal stuff?"

"Eventually, yes. Of course. Albert was stubborn as a mule, but he loved Emma and Rex like they were his own kids. He certainly would have blustered and complained at first, but his heart was always in the right place. The family was everything to him." Thomas gazed off across the room, lost in memories. "We didn't always see eye to eye. Albert could be controlling at times and quick to anger. But whenever I needed help, he was there."

"If that's really who he was, it's hard to imagine him cutting Beatrice out of the will. Or leaving the radio station to someone threatening to expose the paranormal world." I kept my tone light, hoping to set him at ease. "You'd hinted at what Eddie was and what Albert would learn here this weekend. Right?"

"Yes." Thomas missed a step, stiffness bleeding into his frame and grip. His smile remained fixed in place, but it had grown sharp. "You make a fair point, Astra, and it doesn't make sense. Beatrice and Albert fought like cats and dogs, but he was like that girl's father, and if he did leave the station to someone who wasn't family, that wouldn't be like Albert. He was overly generous, if anything, especially where the family was concerned. And he would never have knowingly put Emma or the rest of us in danger." His brow furrowed, and he looked down. "You may be right that something is off here."

I paused, pondering how much to reveal. "Can I ask you a personal question?"

"Sure."

"What would you have done if Albert was gay?" I asked.

Thomas sighed, giving my shoulder a squeeze. "Albert was gay. I always knew, in a way, but we never spoke of it directly. He had his reasons for keeping that part of himself private." A wan smile appeared. "In hindsight, he was not always as discreet as he imagined. I don't know why he never told me, but I always knew. I respected his desire to pretend I didn't."

"You knew?"

"Of course. He was my brother, Astra. That man, Simon—he was Albert's partner. I'm sure of it. Had been for years. I welcomed him as family when Albert chose to bring him around. Which wasn't often, mind you. I loved him as family loves—without condition or judgment. I didn't judge him, and when I told him about Rex and Eddie a couple of weeks ago, he didn't judge me."

I looked up at the big man. "What, exactly, did you tell him?"

"Albert always had an inkling, you know. That the world was not quite what it seemed." A wry smile crossed his face, directed at some memory known only to him. "He suspected there were more things in heaven and earth than were dreamed of in our philosophy. I was always much more pragmatic than he was. Ultimately, I only confirmed as much for Albert—that the paranormal existed and was closer than even he guessed. That I would tell him more at the wedding." Thomas shook his head. "Maybe I shouldn't have told him. Maybe he was stressed and..." His words trailed into pained silence.

"I don't think what you told him..." Then my voice trailed off. Because I really didn't know—

—and then suddenly, I did.

"He didn't die of stress," I said. "That much I know, Mr. Sullivan."

After a moment, Emma's father cleared his throat, defenses rising to veil insight into something lighter. Polite and perfunctory. "Well, what's done is done. No use dwelling on roads not taken or what might have been." He looked down. "How do you think my brother died?"

I sighed, equal parts relief and apprehension. "I think someone went to a lot of trouble to make his death look accidental because they wanted him out of the way." I met Thomas's troubled gaze with a grim one of my own. "The real question is who wanted your brother dead badly enough to kill him and try framing it as an accident. That's what I've been trying to answer. And thanks to you, I think I may know."

* * *

EMMA'S FATHER uttered not a word in response.

He simply nodded, arms falling back to his sides, and moved away from me without saying anything more, as if he knew I suddenly had things to do and people to see.

I watched him make his way across the room to rejoin Elizabeth at their table, her brows furrowing in question at his expression. But Thomas shook his head faintly, dredging up a smile to reassure her, and then leaned forward to hold the baby.

He didn't ask me who I thought had killed his brother.

I scanned the room, spotting Lothian sitting alone at a corner table, nursing a drink. His gaze lifted as I approached, a guarded smile appearing.

"Mind if I join you?" I asked.

"I never mind if you join me." He gestured at the empty chair. "Please."

I plopped down, fingers drumming an

impatient beat on the tablecloth. "So listen, I'm pretty sure I've figured out who offed—"

"Are you ever going to give me the time of day?" he interjected without warning.

I blinked at the abrupt question, stunned. Then I waved it off with a shake of my head. "Look, forget that. I think I know who killed Albert."

"I will not forget—" Lothian's brows shot up. "Wait, you what?"

"I think I solved it. Maybe. Well, Thomas helped, actually." I leaned forward, lowering my voice. "Thomas knew Albert was gay and had a long term partner in Simon. He repeatedly harped about how accepting a family they were, and that included Albert—considering they have a vampire son and a werewolf son-in-law and grandson, I'd say that's pretty plausible, yeah?"

"Sure, but—"

"I'm not done. Thomas said Albert always suspected the paranormal world existed and had an open mind about it. So when Thomas recently confirmed the truth for his brother, Albert didn't freak out. He just accepted it." I paused. "Almost like he already knew." I paused again. "He didn't freak out?" I looked him in the eye, and my arms opened dramatically as if inviting applause.

I didn't get it.

"Why does that mean you know who killed Albert?"

"Put it together." I held up my hand in a fist. "Albert was always into the paranormal." One finger up. "Albert was devoted to his family even though some people didn't think so because of the inheritance thing with his brother." Two fingers up. "He said something about a pack to you that first night—I think he'd already put two and two together just from what Thomas said and that the unveiling would happen at the wedding. I'm sure Emma shacking up with a bunch of men probably helped, too." Three fingers up. "The night Albert died, Connie said Albert was a bit off. Then Vincent told Connie he would check on Albert and repeated that Albert was a bit off. But think about it—they were the only two saying that before Albert was, in fact, a bit off.

Lothian looked at me with an expression of contemplation as if turning my words over carefully in his mind.

"Let me ask you a question," I said. "Did Connie imply she knew what you were when you two were at the pool?"

"I mean, maybe? I don't know. It's possible."

Lothian's expression turned skeptical. "This is all a bit of a leap, though."

"It's not, not considering who Victor is and what he got. I think Victor found out that Albert's family was full of paranormals somehow. Maybe Albert figured it out and told him," I said. "Maybe Aunt Mildred ran her mouth to her daughter, and then Connie told Victor. She certainly didn't strike me as a discrete woman."

"So, if Victor found out…" Lothian frowned. "Oh. Oh, boy. You think that's why Albert suddenly changed his will. Victor found out about the vampires and werewolves in the family and threatened Albert unless he gave him the radio station."

I gave a slow nod. "And once that will is changed, why wait? That way, they could get rid of Albert, make it look natural with dozens of witnesses, and no one would be the wiser—he even made sure his brother was on hand as a paramedic. I'll bet you he's already planning the exposé for his radio show the moment that station is in his hands. Albert Sullivan—murdered by paranormals."

"Why murdered by paranormals?"

"The mushroom pieces were red with white flecks. Do you know what's red with white flecks? Amanita muscaria. Witches use it. It's also sold in apothecaries. So, were they going to frame us? Simon? Who knows."

"That's... pretty dark." Lothian looked around the room, brow furrowed. "Okay, it's a solid theory. I'll give you that. But that's all it is. A theory."

"Yeah, well, maybe not. I have an idea or two about that." I smiled without humor. "Albert Sullivan stuck to the buffet table all night. Prying him from that table would have required the jaws of life."

"Ouch." The werewolf chuckled, then stopped. "That wasn't funny."

"You laughed."

"I shouldn't have."

"Anyway, I just have to find that table and read it. I know that Albert choked on quiche. He also swallowed a piece of steak after the quiche because he didn't think he had an allergic reaction; he wasn't allergic to anything he ate as far as he knew—he thought he was choking. Only he wasn't."

"What does that—"

"Someone put a laced quiche on that table for him to grab. I'd bet on it."

Lothian studied me for a long moment,

expression still dubious. But gradually, his features relaxed, and he gave a curt nod. "All right. If you've really solved this, tell me what we need to do next. If you're right, we're all at risk."

His use of "we" didn't escape my notice. "Let's go find that my father."

* * *

I FOUND THE TABLE.

I saw what I needed to see.

And I invited the unsuspecting couple to the party.

Victor strode through the club doors, an aura of bluster and ego preceding him. But his eyes betrayed him, darting about with wonder and no small amount of gleeful greed—a child with sudden permission to ransack the candy store.

Connie trailed in his wake, lips pursed as if she'd sucked on something bitter. She clutched his arm with white-knuckled anxiety, her gaze fixed upon each step as though making her way through a minefield.

The music stopped. Everyone stared.

"Connie, honey, what are you doing here?" Aunt Mildred asked, confused.

I yelled out a friendly greeting to Connie and

rushed over to grab her hand as if we were long-lost friends. A flood of images surged through my mind—Connie and Victor plotting, arguing over whether to expose the Sullivans and the supernatural before or after the wedding. Victor ranting that he didn't want to wait for the radio station and insisting they'd gain the werewolf pack's wealth, too, if they killed Albert first and then exposed everyone.

She snatched her hand from mine as if my touch were poison, staring around wildly like a mouse trapped by snakes with no escape.

"It was them," I told the guests. "Connie and Victor plotted to kill Albert. He wanted to expose us on his show and hoped to steal the pack's money after he did it."

Gasps erupted around us. All eyes swung to the newcomers.

"You truly believe I came here without considering this might be an ambush?" Victor whipped out a pistol from inside his jacket and aimed it squarely at my chest. "Not one step closer!"

Well, slap me silly. A gun. How positively frightening.

I had to fight the urge not to roll my eyes so hard that I risked straining an optic nerve.

For all Victor fancied himself an expert in matters of the occult and supernatural, the truth was... he didn't know jack about squat. If he did, he would have realized he'd been outgunned even with all of us unarmed.

And we were not all unarmed.

Lothian lunged at Victor with a snarl fit to curdle milk, but Emma shoved him out of the way with a grunt of impatience. Before you could say "shotgun wedding," she had whipped out her pistol and had it trained on Victor. "You wrecked my wedding and killed my uncle, you absolute turnip. Consider yourself fortunate we don't just decide you're the band's dinner."

"Oh, yeah?" Victor grinned, though it didn't reach his eyes. "Go ahead. I'm live streaming all of this. The whole world already knows you're here. Monsters, the lot of you!"

"No live streams are coming from this building," Rex told him.

"It's my phone! I know what my phone is doing!"

Rex strode forward, gesturing toward a large black box at the top of the wall near the ceiling. "That is a jammer. It blocks all signals in or out whenever I decide it should."

Emma aimed a stern look at the vampire. "Those are illegal, Rex."

Rex gave a casual shrug of unconcern. "Are they?"

"You're all freaks!" Victor shrieked. His gun swung wildly between Emma and Rex. "Unnatural beasts that should be put down!"

Connie grabbed Victor's arm, eyes wide with panic. "Victor, stop it! This has gone too far. Let's just leave, please!"

Tears rolled down Aunt Mildred's face. "Connie, honey, is it true? Were you really part of killing your—"

"Shut up, old woman!" Victor snarled, shaking Connie off with a snarl. "This is your fault. You and your damned mother couldn't keep your mouths shut!" Victor jabbed the gun at Rex again. "Back off, bloodsucker, or I'll put a bullet in your heart!"

"I wouldn't if I were you," Emma told him ominously. Eddie stood beside her, silent and menacing.

Victor let out a harsh bark of laughter. "Are you insane? Are you still human after giving birth to that monster's little monster?"

Hunter giggled in Elizabeth's arms. Then he burped.

"Victor, drop the gun," Emma said. "It's over. You're not getting out of here."

"Oh, yeah? Just watch me! The only good paranormal is a dead one!" He pointed the gun at Hunter. "Starting with the newest one of you!"

I don't know why he thought that would be a good move.

But he did.

Evil people don't necessarily equal smart people.

Faster than you could say bang, a towering silhouette hurtled out of nowhere to T-bone Victor at flank speed. A gunshot rang out, exploding one of the overhead lights in a hail of glass shrapnel, and pandemonium ensued as guests erupted into startled bellows and squeals, frantically stumbling over each other in a tangle of flailing limbs, some running away and some leaping toward the gunman—despite the falling glass suspending itself in the air above everyone's heads.

My father smiled reassuringly.

When the action stopped, Lothian had Victor pinned to the floor, the gun now in his werewolf brother Wyatt's grip. Victor bucked and thrashed, spewing obscenities, as Lothian held him down.

The werewolf growled, wrenching Victor's arms behind his back.

Out of nowhere, a familiar dulcet tone cut through the tension in the room like a chainsaw through butter. "For goodness' sake. You people can't stay out of trouble for a single week, can you?"

I looked up.

Chief Daniel Harmon came swaggering in, tucking his service weapon back into its holster with a noise of mild irritation. He surveyed the room's current chaos and mayhem with an expression caught between faint annoyance and resignation before turning to Emma. "And you wondered why I never bothered to RSVP to this shindig?"

# CHAPTER NINETEEN

Strings of fairy lights twinkled throughout the club, bathing everything in a soft golden glow. A mixing of mortal and supernatural guests filled the space, some seated at tables and others mingling, all facing the small stage where Emma and Eddie stood hand in hand before Apollo.

My father smiled benevolently at the couple, the stage lights glinting off his tawny hair. "Friends and family, we have come together on this most joyous of occasions to commemorate a love that blossomed in the face of immense hardships on the battlefield of a war across the world."

Apollo's words elicited a loud sniffle from

Elizabeth Sullivan's sister, Aunt Mildred. I glanced over to find her dabbing at her eyes with a handkerchief, leaning against Uncle Buddy.

Despite the craziness of the last twenty-four hours, the wedding was still on.

My father's sonorous voice rang clear through Sanguine, each word etched with care. "Today, we celebrate the union of two kindred spirits who were determined enough, brave enough, to rise above every tribulation thrown their way, unbending in their resolve to find their way back into the arms of the other."

A wry whisper tickled my ear as Ami leaned in, her lips so close they almost grazed my skin. "Quite diplomatic of him to omit the part where Emma orchestrated most of those tribulations."

"Hush now," Althea chided Ami. "We're bridesmaids. We vowed not to snark on the bride today, no matter how much she may deserve it. Zip the lip."

Emma briefly glared at us before turning back to my father.

Her own father, Thomas, gave her a watery smile from the front row as he patted his wife's hand. "So beautiful and strange," he whispered. "Who's have thought we'd have such amazing things in our lives, Lizzie?"

"Thomas, hush. You can ruminate later." Elizabeth cuddled little Hunter as he cooed. "Let them get married before Emma changes her mind."

"Mom!"

"The path of true love never did run smooth," Apollo continued as if none of us had ever interrupted, hints of wryness coloring his tone. "But for those willing to brave the dark forests and face inner and outer demons, eternal love awaits."

Eddie gazed at his bride, eyes gleaming almost gold in the stage lights, expression so full of devotion and wonder it made my heart ache.

After everything, they'd found their way here.

They deserved this moment.

Emma gazed up at him in turn, joyful tears slipping free to trail down her cheeks. But her smile was radiant as the sun, filled with the promise of new beginnings.

And in that smile, I glimpsed hope for us all.

Apollo smiled at me and then at Lothian, who stood beside Eddie as best man. "The maid of honor and the best man are vital to the bridal party, offering their love and support. At the request of the bride and groom, and as they are both single, I offer a benediction: May their own path lead them to find what their two friends have found."

It took every ounce of restraint I possessed not to plant my fist right in the middle of each of their smug mugs in the middle of Emma's wedding.

My gaze met Lothian's, a flush creeping up my neck at my father's thinly veiled hint. We had come a long way, Lothian and I.

Once upon a time, I'd considered him an annoyance at best—a cocky werewolf far too sure of his charm and appeal and opinions. But time and circumstance had revealed hidden depths I never expected.

Depths that continued to draw me in even when I would've preferred to remain blissfully oblivious.

Lothian had proven himself in the aftermath of Albert's death, his steadfast support giving me a lifeline when emotions threatened to overwhelm me. And though we continued to butt heads occasionally, those moments were infused with a warmth and affection that caught me by surprise.

A part of me was reluctant to crack open the door for anything deeper to take root.

Yet every once in a while, in Lothian's smile, I

caught a fleeting glimpse of what life might hold in store if I finally found the courage to stop running scared. A future I realized in the middle of Emma's pink twinkly wedding that maybe, just maybe, I wasn't quite so afraid to face after all.

Apollo spread his arms wide, drawing all eyes back to the bride and groom. "Emma and Eddie have prepared their own vows to share on this special day. Eddie, you may begin."

Eddie took Emma's hands, gazing deep into her eyes. "Emma, from the moment I saw you, I knew you were my soulmate, my destiny, the one I wanted to share forever with." His voice grew hoarse with emotion. "You saw beyond the soldier to the man within, and your love gives me the strength and courage to become better each and every day. I vow to love and protect you and our children, to support your dreams as you have supported mine, and to share eternity by your side."

Emma blinked back tears, smiling up at him tremulously. "Eddie, you opened my eyes to love I never imagined was real or possible. You accept me as I am, see my truth, and bring out the best in me." She squeezed his hands. "I vow to stand by your side, to love you with all my heart, and to continue building a life together with you and our children filled with joy, passion, and adventure."

Apollo raised his hands over the couple, a glow of power shimmering just faint enough to be noticeable if the mortals looked closely. "With the exchange of eternal vows and the gods' blessing upon you, I now pronounce you husband and wife. You may kiss—"

Eddie swept Emma into his arms and kissed her before Apollo could finish speaking. Laughter and cheers erupted from the guests, myself included.

When the happy couple finally surfaced from their bubble of newlywed kissy-faced bliss for a breath of air, Emma spun on her heel without warning and lobbed her bouquet straight at me like a grenade. I scrambled to catch the thing, clutching the flowers in stunned disbelief.

Emma flashed a grin, winking. "You're next!"

I peeked over to Lothian to find him rubbing the back of his neck, a hint of color on his cheeks but eyes lit with humor.

Apollo chuckled, drawing my gaze. "Out of the mouths of babes and brides..." His expression sobered. "The future is unwritten, Daughter. What path do you choose to walk?"

"The one that leads to the bar," I told him and stepped off the dais.

* * *

THE RECEPTION WAS in full swing, with guests mingling and drinking champagne while the (mortal) band played soft jazz. I stood to the side, watching Emma and Eddie share their first dance, lost in their own world.

"Quite the shindig."

I turned to find Chief Harmon beside me, a glass of champagne in hand. He gave me a nod of greeting. "Despite the madness of the past few days, it looks like they got their perfect day after all."

"Glad you could make it after all." I glanced past him, expecting to see Lillian, but she wasn't there. My brow furrowed. "She didn't come?"

He sighed. "She was happy to pass on what she learned from Albert's ghost about what Victor and Connie had done and were planning to do," he said, "but she's still struggling where you're concerned. It's progress. A month ago, she would have let all of you get exposed by that murderous shock jock and been done with everyone."

"Well, glad to hear about that progress," I supplied wryly.

Harmon's looked down at me. "Astra, it will take some time, but I think she'll get there. It was her only son, and she didn't see it coming. It hurt her on many levels. As a mother, as a psychic, as Cassandra's leader." He took a sip of his drink. "She's coming around gradually."

"I can't do anything but wait."

"At least she doesn't want to shoot you anymore."

My gaze strayed back to Emma and Eddie, still lost in their own world. "I know she thinks I didn't care about him, but I really did think Jason and I would marry someday."

"Which would have been an unmitigated catastrophe, if I'm being frank."

I blinked at him. "I beg your pardon?"

"You're an ex-military witch, and he was a nice schoolteacher from Central Florida. Don't get me wrong, I think you two cared about each other, but long term? It was never going to work." Harmon sipped his champagne. "Have you met his girlfriend in the underworld? She's delightful and a much better fit for him."

"Color me stunned by your unvarnished candor," I informed him, hastily steering the conversation into less choppy waters. "Did you guys arrest the paramedic De Luca brother?"

"You have to ask?" Harmon glanced at me sidelong. "For all their complicated plots, conspiracy theories, and long-game plans, those three were like any other criminals. Stupid, greedy, and quick to turn on one another for self-preservation." Harmon took a slow, circumspect sip of his drink. "Cousin Connie sang like a canary once her lawyer showed up. She gave up the De Lucas and their plot in less than an hour."

"No kidding."

"And you were right—Mildred told her daughter about the werewolves and got the whole thing rolling. Connie told her crazy boyfriend, and he went after Albert. Turns out he knew that Albert was keeping Simon a secret and could use that—and the threat of exposing Emma and Rex's family—to get what he wanted." He looked at me. "Was your father able to Men in Black everybody that needed to be?"

One of my father's many talents (thanks to being a god and all) is the ability to simply reach in and extract memories straight from someone's mind, kind of like picking cherries right off a tree. It's technically a healing power.

Anyway, before Chief Harmon called in the

rest of the police cavalry the previous night, Apollo made quick work of ensuring any non-essential personnel Emma and Eddie had seen fit to induct into the 'paranormals are real, and the gods walk among us' club got a swift mental scrub and shoved right back outside the inner circle—starting with Aunt Mildred and Uncle Buddy.

It's safer for humans not to know about the paranormal world.

Safer for us.

Safer for them.

Emma's heart was in the right place, wanting to come clean with select kin about their furry little situation and who Hunter really was. But secrets being what they are, they inevitably turn up where they're not meant to be, and it was obvious from this situation that some knowledge was just too dangerous to leave unrestrained.

Harmon's expression grew serious. "There's something else you might want to know. Albert's original will was reinstated by a judge today, considering it was clear he made the new one under duress. Beatrice inherited the radio station after all."

Huh. I wasn't sure how to feel about that. Beatrice seemed nearly as angry and vindictive as

Victor in her own way. Was that situation really any better?

Before I could voice the thought, Simon wandered over to join us.

I'd shared with Thomas that Simon was in town, and Mr. Sullivan had reached out to the man Albert had kept hidden from the family for their entire relationship. They'd had a long talk, Emma said, and while they weren't sure why Albert never trusted his family with his truth, Thomas was determined to welcome the man into the family as he should have been welcomed from the beginning.

He gave me a nod of greeting, then turned to Chief Harmon. "I wanted to thank you again for your help in resolving this whole mess."

Harmon shook Simon's hand. "You're most welcome. I'm just glad this story seems to have a satisfactory ending. Things being set right and all that."

"Beatrice got the station," I said. I couldn't quite keep the doubt from my tone.

"I'm sure what you overheard in that dinner doesn't make you think very well of the young woman." Simon smiled gently. "But Bea has had a hard life and has a hard time accepting love when it's offered. Albert never stopped trying, you know, and now..." His smile turned bittersweet. "Now she has no choice but to do something good with the gift he left her. I hope in time she comes to see it for the gesture of love it was meant to be."

I eyed him with surprise. How could he be so forgiving toward someone so spiteful? But Simon merely gazed back, serene understanding in his eyes. "If you say so," I told him.

"Sometimes the hardest hearts to reach are the ones most in need of love," he said simply. "And sometimes love means not giving up, even when faced with anger and rejection—or even just simple attitude. Albert was that lesson for me. I hope Beatrice comes to learn it as well in the days ahead."

He nodded politely and wandered off to mingle with other guests.

* * *

LOTHIAN SWEPT me onto the dance floor as the band struck up a ballad fit for swaying in close quarters. Ignoring the jitterbugs protesting in my stomach, I looped my arms around his neck while his hands came to rest against my waist, radiating heat through the thin material of my (pink) dress.

"How is Aunt Mildred here?" he wondered aloud. "I'd have thought she'd be a mess with Connie in jail."

"Connie folded like a lawn chair the second the police said 'prison,' and thanks to that table's ability to retain memories, the police know—well, Harmon knows—Victor was the one that pawned that dodgy quiche on Albert, and the paramedic brother worked to cover it up. So maybe it's good she gets the deal for flipping."

Lothian's brows shot up. "She was the one who told Victor to lace it with walnuts, though. And she's a nurse."

"Yeah, well, I don't care. They were all caught. That's all I care about. Let the system sort them out." My gaze drifted over his shoulder to where Emma and Eddie were still dancing, lost in their own world. "They look so cute together. But I swear, if I see anything pink again for the next year, I will zap it into another dimension with my magic fingers."

"Speaking of caught..." Lothian nodded pointedly at the bouquet still tucked under my arm. "You still haven't answered my question." His voice dropped to a husky whisper as he inched closer, a roguish smile playing on his lips.

"Are you ever going to give me the time of day, Astra?"

I averted my gaze as the heat rose in my cheeks, suddenly intensely aware of the delicate pink rose petals brushing my skin. "It's almost ten at night. There. You have the time of day." I slid a glance at him sideways. The gleam of determination in his eyes told me he had no intention of being brushed off again. "No?"

"No."

"Look. Relationships don't come easy for me, Lothian. The easy ones are where I don't feel too much, you know? Where I can approach things intellectually. Rationally." I moistened my lips, at a loss for a rebuttal witty enough to mask the effect his proximity had on me. "When there are intense feelings, I tend to… run away from them."

"I see." Lothian's eyes drifted pointedly to the bouquet still nestled in the crook of my arm, and then he looked me in the eye. "Are you running away now?"

"No, I just…" The words snagged in my throat as I grappled for a way to explain the fortifications I'd spent a lifetime constructing— and why I wasn't yet ready to dismantle them stone by stone.

A smile flickered at the edges of Lothian's

mouth as understanding dawned in his eyes. "It's all right. I know a thing or two about walls myself." His fingers reached up to brush a stray lock from my cheek, tucking it gently behind my ear. "How about this—you keep giving me pieces of yourself, as and when you're able. And I'll keep putting them together until you realize there's no need for barriers between us at all."

"I...I think I can do that." The words slipped out, tremulous yet hopeful. I wet my lips, wavering. "Well. Maybe."

A low laugh rumbled in his chest at my vacillation as he nodded in acquiescence. "Maybe is enough for me—for now. Maybe is a start. It's better than no." His fingers slipped from my cheek, but his penetrating gaze remained. "I'm a patient man, Astra. My offer stands for whenever you're ready. I'll still be here."

Lothian laughed and drew me into his arms without a word, our foreheads touching as the song ended. Lothian pulled back to look down at me, humor, affection, and a promise of patience in his eyes. "So, when's our first date?"

"That's your idea of patience?"

"You're going to be a handful, Astra Arden. Aren't you?" A crooked grin and a glint in his eye seemed oddly warm and rich with meaning.

"I have no idea what you mean."

"Yes, you do." Lothian leaned in close, his whisper raising goosebumps on my skin. "And you know what? I'm looking forward to it." With a parting smile, he turned and strode into the crowd, leaving my heart racing with anticipation.

Walls that had long shielded me now seemed more like a cage holding me back from all that might be. The seeds of 'maybe' Lothian had sown were already working their slow magic within.

* * *

## THANK YOU FOR READING!

I hope you enjoyed **Of Owl the Nerve**. Please think about leaving a review! Astra, Archie and the whole Arden family continue their adventures in Book 14, Owl Out of Magic.

# KEEP UP WITH LEANNE LEEDS

Thanks so much for reading! I hope you liked it! Want to keep up with me?

Visit leanneleeds.com to:

Find all my books…

Sign up for my newsletter…

Like me on Facebook…

Follow me on Twitter…

Follow me on Instagram…

Thanks again for reading!

Leanne Leeds

# FIND A TYPO? LET US KNOW!

Typos happen. It's sad, but true.

Though we go over the manuscript multiple times, have editors, have beta readers, and advance readers it's inevitable that determined typos and mistakes sometimes find their way into a published book.

Did you find one? If you did, think about reporting it on leanneleeds.com so we can get it corrected.

# ARTIFICIAL INTELLIGENCE STATEMENT

Portions of this book were created with the assistance of AI tools used for editing, proofreading, and refining the text. However, the ideas, storyline, characters, and overall creative vision remain my own original work.

While some aspects of the cover image were generated using AI tools, it was done so under my creative direction and curation.

I want to acknowledge the use of these technologies as part of my creative process, while affirming that the essence of this work comes from my own imagination and effort.

Leanne Leeds

Made in the USA
Las Vegas, NV
05 December 2023

82125152R00194